NO WAY OUT

PX DUKE

No Way Out

A Frank Ross Road Trip

More Frank Ross Road Trips

Midnight at the Oasis
Bank Robber Dames
Fast Food Slow Waitress
Bad Girls

Print Books

Jim Nash The Beginning
Gun Crazy
Gun Crazy 2
Gun Crazy 3
Fallen Angels
Last Stop to Nowhere
Revenge Is Justice
Escape / Forget Me Not
Wedding Bell Blues / Breakdown
Mexico Time
No Free Ride / Gone

Dead Reckoning
Uncharted
Go-Around
Sand Storm

No Way Out
Bad Girls
Bank Robber Dames

The Last President

Some of this could be true.

Prologue

It must have been quite a sight in 1905 when the Colorado River burst the levees near Yuma and overran towns and farms and a railroad in the Salton basin. By the time the burst banks were repaired, the expanse of water created in the basin was forty miles long and thirteen miles wide. It covered four hundred square miles.

When it was all over and the damage was done, the water remained behind. It couldn't drain south into the Sea of Cortez or north into the L.A. Basin. There was nowhere for the water to go, then or now.

They began calling it the Salton Sea, but it wasn't much of one. At most, it was fifty feet deep in places, and more likely thirty feet on average. At 225 feet below sea level, it was just five feet higher than Death Valley's lowest elevation.

The Salton Sea thrived. During the late 50s, the developers couldn't resist. They moved in to take advantage of the location to create a recreation and resort destination. Yacht clubs, marinas, restaurants and nightclubs all vied for the attention of the rich and famous that came to escape big-city L.A. to the north. Like moths to a flame, they were drawn to the excitement on their newly discovered California Riviera.

The party didn't last long.

In the early 70s, heavy rains created runoff, and floods damaged the area. The coastline towns and resorts were flooded and re-flooded when water levels rose. To add insult to injury, not one but two hurricanes swept through and the flame was finally, permanently, blown out.

People walked, ran and drove away. Eventually, almost everything was closed and abandoned. Only scattered junk remained behind to be salvaged by anyone who chose to stay, or by those who wanted to escape El Lay and move to the isolation of the dilapidated, rusting former resort towns located on the shore of the Salton Sea.

In summer, daytime temperatures often hit triple digits, and the nights aren't far behind. The once-successful resort area is only a faint memory for the old-timers scattered around the Salton Sea. The towns are mostly deserted, populated only by the few regulars who have remained long past their best-before dates. They live in broken-down trailers and houses built in the 60s when times were good.

In a place such as this, the dream died fast and hard a long time ago.

$$\boxed{1}$$

Ihit the road running hard every September. It could be a little later, depending on where I was when the fall weather hit. Cold, rain, sleet, and snow were too familiar to the people that never left. I became fed up with it on a regular basis and bugged out on a whim and cold morning dew that would turn too fast to frost.

I wasn't looking for much. I followed the retreating warm weather on the hunt for a place to park and a roof that didn't leak. I tried on the Florida Keys for a while, but that turned out to be a giant snooze-fest. Eventually, I rode west to southern California. It fast became my temporary refuge of choice.

By the time late spring arrived, it would be time to hurry home to see what I missed. Usually it amounted to not much of anything. Over time, I became unable to turn away from the siren call of California and the seductive warmth she offered up that resembled the warm, sweet insides of a willing woman's thighs.

There was always a problem with things like that,

though. As with returning to a buffet table too many times, one could often get too much of a good thing. So I deserted her and wondered why it took me so long.

Mexico next became my favorite place to spend a winter. It wasn't the mainland that appealed to me. The more isolated states of Baja, California—*Norte y Sur*—were the ones that beckoned.

Fickle as I was, I chose them both, one after the other. The pattern was as random as only a single paved road running up and down the length of the peninsula for a thousand miles could provide.

The winter sun danced on the Sea of Cortez. The locals called it the Golfo de California. Blue sky, sunshine, warm weather and friendly, unassuming locals made for an enjoyable stay. Occasionally, I'd encounter a kind woman, local or imported, who would offer to help while away the hours and keep me warm in the darkness of short winter nights.

The beer I liked—*Sol*—wasn't so bad, either.

I discovered Playa Bonita while on a ride to Puertecitos on the Sea of Cortez. Someone graded a trail over the sand in the direction of the gulf. Out of boredom, I turned off the main road. At the end of the trail, I discovered a bar with a pool table and a second-floor patio. It allowed me to sit and enjoy an early-morning Sol while gazing across the Golfo and to wait for the sunrise.

My tent found a home on a cement pad under a palapa and I was happy. The closest neighbor, when there was one, was a hundred and fifty feet away. To say I was content would have been an understatement.

The playa was so out of the way it never became swamped with RVs full of Hawaiian-shirt gabachos trying to recapture long-lost youth. The poor trail over drifting beach sand probably helped with that. Capable four-wheel drives overloaded with college kids often showed up during spring break.

That's when I would make a run for it. I'd break camp and disappear completely, headed for the border in a run for the summer up north. Not always, though. Sometimes I'd go scarce for only a week. Sometimes, if I was late to leave, I'd get an occasional spring breaker who wanted to investigate. I'd smoke her dope and feed her booze and cook for her, and if she stayed around for a few days, I was happy.

If not, I didn't care. Easy come. Easy go.

Either way, I would pack up and be gone after a winter spent drinking good beer and wasting away. I didn't mind. I never did. Better that than shovel snow and grow old doing it.

Crossing la línea—the border—on the way home was never a problem. The drug dogs on patrol never looked cross-eyed at me. I would lower my sunglasses in advance so the whites of my eyes were plainly visible to the border guard. I'd plant a grin on my face, and tell him, *I'm just happy to be here.*

It worked every time. It brought a chuckle followed by a knowing shake of the head and a wave-through with nary a question. A stop for fuel in Calexico followed by another in Indio, and from there I'd be home-free.

I got on the road long before sunup. I wanted to kill miles in the cool, early-morning desert air. I was running hard to get as far north as I could in a single day. Come mid-morning, I needed a break from the dust and dirt and monotony that was kicking me in the gut as only four-lane blacktop can do.

I was seventy miles north of the border and I was looking for a pull-off, somewhere with a gas-and-go. Across the highway in the distance I caught a reflection. The brand-new casino grew bigger and brighter in the mid-morning sunshine. It had to be calling my name. I never could resist a siren's call, no matter who or what was doing the calling.

On a whim I downshifted, changed lanes and hit the binders to make the turnoff into the welcoming oasis. I figured on taking a quick break. I wanted to get something to chew on that I wouldn't have to choke down with cheese for good luck. Coming hot out of a winter spent in Mexico will do that sometimes.

My bagger was running good. Maybe too good, if that was possible. I prided myself on that. I ran many hundreds, sometimes a thousand miles, on any day when I was trying to make time and distance. Today was one of those days. I was well on my way to hitting that thousand.

After taking on a full tank, I moved to park on the shady side of the building and walked around front to enter the air-conditioned splendor. I grabbed a quick cheese and chicken chimi—a chimichanga—and a water and settled in to enjoy my break in the cool air. I didn't burn any daylight, though. I was back on the road in twenty minutes and ready to turn north onto the 86.

Fickle lady that luck was known to be, she deserted me as I pulled out of the parking lot to get back on the road. My cranny slipped a gear. The engine revved. I was done for dinner and stranded, a little better than half-way up the west side of the Salton Sea. In the middle of nowhere.

If it wasn't nowhere, somebody should take the time to explain why.

I manhandled the bike back to the shady side of the gas-n-go and opened up my tools. I tried a couple of things to get back on the road. No luck. Like I said, fickle lady luck deserted me. I stowed my tools and took a look around the fresh asphalt in the parking lot. Waves of heat rose with the exhaust from idling semis lined up in rows with cabin air on full.

My bad luck started to turn a little better when I spied the flatbed tow-truck languishing in a deserted corner of the lot. If I was real lucky, I wouldn't end up getting hosed by a call-out fee.

I wandered over and placed a hand on a cold hood. The driver had to be inside, probably trying to hit it big. All I had to do was wait him out. I was betting on a long wait, and sure enough, it was long enough. Either the driver had been busy re-investing his winnings or he was independently wealthy.

He walked out and squinted into the early afternoon sunlight and the heat radiating in waves off the fresh asphalt. He made for the flatbed and I took my cue. I caught up just as he opened the door to climb into the cab. I felt like a puppy glad to see anyone. Desperation would have been a better name for it, but I was never going to admit that.

The driver—Billy according to the name embroidered on his powder-blue shirt—was quick to work out a cash deal. Satisfied, he backed up to my ride and tilted the bed. He let me hook up to my front forks. I balanced the bike as the driver winched it onto the flatbed.

I figured there was no sense wasting space. I maneuvered my ride sideways, working it in close to the cab, and tied down. Billy had enough room left for a small car. If he got another call he'd make a little more cash to fund his next trip to the casino.

So much for the bike.

Most everything I rode past after crossing the border was closed, abandoned or rusted junk—and for me, that included Calexico and El Centro. The flatbed driver mentioned a motel a couple of miles up the road. He wasn't ready to abandon the casino just yet. He made arrangements for one of his casino compatriots to drop me off on the way and went back in to the casino to spend his new-found riches.

I tossed my bag on the floor of the half-ton free taxi ride and got in. The surly driver barely uttered word one on the four-lane drive north. He must have been thinking he'd be better spending his time and his money back at the casino. He turned east off the highway into town, and I knew right away I was somewhere I didn't want to be.

Calling the place a town was generous. Empty desert landscape surrounded vacant subdivision lots fronted by paved streets. It resembled a real-estate development on hold. Taken by the absurdity of it, I never thought to ask questions. The driver halted at a beat-up, single-story motel.

The Palms wasn't much, but it was enough for me. It almost overlooked the sea. It would have if a second story had been added when it was built back in the 60s. Now it looked to be barely hanging on in a place that long ago had passed its own best-before date.

I opened the door to the office and checked into nowhere to get a key. Okay, technically it wasn't exactly nowhere, but it was close enough. I could still be on the south side of the border down Mexico way with a broke-down motorcycle and no place to park.

That would be nowhere.

New bath towels. Fancy comforters. Well-lit parking in ten paved stalls. All that according to the brochure on the front desk. What a draw. If I needed to hide, this was definitely the place.

I walked into my room. Cranked up the window shaker. Turned on the water in the showers and ran through on slow to get wet. I dried off with one of the advertised new bath towels. Cool air was drumming out of the window-shaker. At least it worked, even if it rattled.

I collapsed on the bed and fell into an exhausted sleep. I dreamed of being back on the road first thing in the morning. I didn't bother to get up in the middle of the night to check on which part of the parking lot was well-lit.

I was just happy to be here.

First thing in the morning, the flatbed growled into the motel parking lot. I stepped out into the low sun to greet it. The driver would have figured I wasn't going anywhere. I climbed onto the tipping flatbed and slid down beside the bike until both wheels rested on solid ground.

"Fifty cash ought to cover it," Billy, the driver, said. He hadn't unfastened my front forks yet. Maybe thought I was going to skip out and ride off into the sunrise and the Salton Sea.

I already paid the man in the casino parking lot. How much money did this guy lose at the casino's single table? "Fifty? Shit, I could've pushed it here for that."

"You want the bike or not? This time, when I drag it up the bed I'll be sure it's on its side. You won't need to help."

"No, don't do that." I grinned a nervous grin and reached into a back pocket. "Thanks for everything." I counted out the fifty like it was the last cash wasting away in my pocket. It nearly was. I figured he'd be back at the casino burning that fifty in a Las Vegas minute. On a whim I added another ten to the thin roll and handed it to him.

You never know.

"Thanks. Are you good now?" Billy the tow-truck driver asked as his flatbed whirred.

I was. "You bet. I'm going to hunker down until a friend does his thing and ships me some parts."

"You could do worse than this place," Billy said. "It's clean. Not too far from a place to eat. You might even get lucky and find a ride to the casino for a change of scenery.

"I'll keep that in mind." I could use the place to eat, too.

If I was able to, I would have escaped at sunup in the cool of the desert morning. Not so this time. I was trapped. And now I was leaning against a rusty neon signpost, killing time watching a flatbed leave town and wanting to be on the road right behind it.

It was the best I could hope for at The Palms Motel in Bombay Shores.

2

I heard it before I saw it. The beater rumbled and rattled its way into the parking lot. The well-lit parking lot, according to the brochure I snagged from the front desk. The lonely overhead light was still on, too. Except it was morning, so I guess the parking lot was well lit after all.

The driver bumped her shoulder against a door hanging on rusty hinges. They squeaked and she wrestled it open. The driver swiveled in the seat and put two feet on the pavement. She straightened and managed to push-slam the door closed with an errant swing of a well-formed hip swaddled in tight jeans.

The dilapidated old car had definitely seen better days. A lot better. The paint was faded by too many years under desert sun and salt-laden sea air. The windows were all down, probably because the air conditioner stopped working sometime in the last ten years.

All right, so calling it a beater was too kind.

I stood my ground leaning against the motel

signpost and waited for her to walk past to the office. I took a nice long drink with eyes shaded by dark glasses. I looked down and up and back down again just because I could. I couldn't help it. I never could.

I smiled because I liked what I saw. If it annoyed her, I didn't care.

I pushed my sunglasses over my forehead. Hers kept me from getting a look at her eyes. I liked to see their eyes. You can tell a lot about someone from the eyes.

Up close she wasn't anything special. No makeup. Thin lips. Small breasts. But she had dark hair and behind those sunglasses, I hoped for dark eyes to match the hair. Although, the long, dark hair alone was enough to get me interested.

The bridge of her nose had that little bump on it that always caught my fancy.

This one wasn't a shy one. She almost brushed up against as she went by. I turned to get a fresh look at the other side. Like I would a steak on a grill. I always liked to check both sides.

Even with those flap pockets in the back that make a woman's ass look fat, hers didn't look that way at all. It was nice and tight looking, aided as it was by snug jeans. It was nice enough that I hoped I'd get to see more of it.

That, and I wondered what her legs were like.

I manhandled my ride to the parking spot in front of my room and retrieved my tools from a saddlebag. In no time I had the primary cover off and the clutch loosened up. That was pretty much it until the courier showed up.

I was buttoning everything up to keep the dust out. Shoes scraping sand on asphalt got my attention. I looked up. Whoever it was had me squinting against the sun into a silhouette. Could it be?

"Hello," she said.

Yes, it could. And with a soft, gentle voice. "Hello. You're the woman I saw getting out of the car."

"Yes, that was me."

Things were starting to pick up in these parts. "You staying here?" I asked, as I stood up for a better look.

"No. I make up the rooms."

I looked across the empty expanse of asphalt. "Not too busy today, are you? The well-lit parking lot is almost empty." I grinned up at her.

She grinned back. "You read the brochure. We only had a couple of rooms rented last night. You make three."

Good. She wasn't busy. "It's kind of sleepy here."

"It's okay if you want to escape," she said.

"Are you escaping?" From what I could tell squinting into a shadow, her eyes appeared to move off.

She changed the subject. "You want your room done right now? I can come back later if you like. I live just down the street."

For sure I was interested. "Now would be okay. I'm going to be busy out here for a bit. Let me know when you're finished."

Twenty minutes and she was back. Or maybe it was ten. This time I didn't have to squint to get a look. She made sure she was facing the sun. I took another long drink. I was pretty sure she knew what I was doing, even behind my sunglasses.

"Your room is done," she said.

"Thanks."

She cast a glance in the direction of my ride. I'd say you're going to be here for a while."

She must have talked to the guy at the front desk. Dell, according to the name embroidered on his bowling shirt when I checked in. I wondered where the bowling alley was, but I didn't ask.

"Is there anything else you need?" she asked.

Actually, there was. I needed to see the rest of her. I could use a little bit of alabaster to rub the brown of the Mexicanas off. That wouldn't hurt, either. I didn't say any of it out loud. "Is there a restaurant or a diner close by?" I wasn't holding out hope.

"I'm going to the casino in a bit. You can tag along if you like."

"Sure. Give me a couple to put away my tools and clean up," I said.

We made small talk on the short drive in her beater. She was working at the motel to make enough cash to get farther north. "Then I got stuck here. It could be worse, I guess. At least I have a job."

I never asked how she got stuck. "Lucky you. I'm headed north after spending the winter down Mexico way on the Baja. And I don't have a job."

"And then your bike broke down and now you're stuck here, too." Her voice had a sympathetic tone. Or so it seemed.

"That's pretty much it until I get some parts. I'm stuck in nowhere wasting my cash on a motel room. By the time I get the bike back together I probably won't be able to afford a tank of gas."

She stopped asking questions after that. She probably figured I was just another down-and-out broke-ass biker missing two nickels to rub together. She wouldn't be far wrong, considering my situation. "I'm Frank Ross, by the way. What's yours?"

"Jade Walker."

Well now. I was right about the alabaster. I was proved right about the car's air conditioner, too. The only breeze blew in through the open windows. We pulled into the casino's parking lot and I unstuck myself from the seat. I stepped out into the high-noon sun burning itself into the casino's fresh-paved, black as night parking lot.

"Do you work here?"

"No. My friend does," Jade said. "Tammi will be getting off her shift in a bit. When you're fed and watered come find me and we'll head back."

I didn't want to miss the ride back. I made my way to the deli counter and wolfed down a sandwich in a hurry. I paid and wandered past the doorway into the small casino. Slots, mostly. A single game table.

The place reeked of tobacco. Most everyone was sucking on a cigarette. I searched the smoky room looking for Jade. I caught her, leaning against a slot. She was deep in conversation with a long, tall, good-looking drink of cool water.

Two for two. Not so bad. My luck on the road seemed to me to have found a sunny side. I approached the pair and conversation ceased in a hurry for an introduction.

Jade introduced her friend. "This is Tammi."

I reached a hand out and she took it. "Tammi Dominga. Pleased to meet you, Frank."

"Jade and I met back at the motel," I told her.

I barely paid attention to the other woman. Jade had my attention, and she knew it when she caught me checking her out while I introduced myself to Tammi. What the hell, she's a woman. She ought to be used to it by now. I let her see my eyes flick over her one more time and then I looked her straight in the eye.

Well, what now, I wondered.

"Tammi and I were talking about going over to my place to hang out and listen to some music. You can come if you like," Jade said.

I could barely hear Jade against the noisy backdrop of the small room. She turned to Tammi and I took another good look, up and down. Still a nice fit in those jeans. She had a bra on under her white blouse, holding just enough to keep my curiosity piqued.

That was okay with me. I liked small-breasted women. They weren't always trying to stick their tits in my face to get what they wanted. They had other ways to do that. Ways I liked a lot more.

"I need to finish up a couple of things on my ride. How about if I show up later?"

Jade didn't take any time considering. "That's okay with me."

Tammi didn't say anything, but I don't think she minded, either. I knew that to be true when she aimed both breasts at me and arched her back. Things were looking way up.

We piled into Jade's beater for the ride back to the deserted town. Tammi took a turn and volunteered her story. Unlike Jade, she was a local girl with no car and high school had been a bus-ride away. After graduating she couldn't wait to blow the desert ghost town. She did a circuit around Southern California, Arizona and New Mexico for a year. When she ran out of cash she took part-time jobs to make up the difference.

I wanted to know more. "What did you work at?"

"Nothing too exciting. Mostly I wanted to see the sights. Working part-time gave me the chance. When I had enough I came home and got lucky when the casino hung a help-wanted sign in the window."

Tammi had to be leaving something out. On the roads I traveled, the only people I knew who did a circuit were carnies, pole dancers and peelers. I left out truck drivers. She didn't look like one. I wondered which of the three she was, but I didn't ask. We all had secrets, and some were anxious to keep them.

"So now you're saving cash for your next adventure."

"Well, I don't know about an adventure," Tammi said. "I had all the adventure I needed after I pulled up stakes the first time. I'm ready to take a break. How long it'll last is anyone's guess."

That sounded good to me. "I know how you feel. I'm itching to get home, too. All I need are some bike parts to make good my escape."

I never asked Tammi if she had a boyfriend. I figured she had a local she went to school with. Next you know she'd be shacked up, knocked up and getting smacked up regularly by her old man on drunken

Saturday nights. On Sunday morning he'd be crying his way to forgiveness at the breakfast table and finding his salvation in church later in the day.

Life goes on. Like I was such a prize.

Broke-ass and stuck in a nowhere town after spending the winter down on the Baja. I was lucky I made it out of Mexico before my bike did its number on me and broke down. At least the ass wasn't torn out of my jeans.

Yet.

I still had a bit of cash in my pocket. Probably enough to get me home if I counted real careful. I was a prize all right.

Jade turned off the highway and pulled into the motel's lot. "When you're ready my place is just down the street toward the sea. You'll see the car out front."

T he air conditioner welcomed me back to my latest home away from home with window-rattling comfort. The man-made breeze proved to be a relief from the oppressive afternoon heated air conditioning of Jade's beater.

I stripped down, washed up and hit the rack for a mid-afternoon siesta. You can't be too careful.

And I'm not getting any younger.

3

It was late afternoon when I came to. I recognized the rattle in the window and opened an eye to confirm I was still where I didn't want to be. The room was a lot warmer than when I passed out, and I wondered what it would be like on a real hot day. I decided I didn't want to be around to find out.

I dove into the shower, turned around to get wet, and stepped out. I dried off with one of the advertised new bath towels. I dug in my bag for the clean clothes I always started with when I headed out on a run.

Satisfied with the new look in the mirror the same as the old look, I headed out hoofing it down the road. I kept an eye out for Jade's beater. There weren't a lot of doors to knock on, but my guess was good. Tammi framed herself in it when she showed up to open it. For spite she turned sideways to show me what I was missing. Turns out it was plenty. She was one good-looking woman. Hell, if I wasn't already interested in Jade I'd be all over her.

She leaned back against the door, forcing me to

walk past her to get in. One at a time, her breasts brushed lightly against my arm. Or maybe I imagined it. For an instant I considered stopping between them. I kept on into the trailer. Or were they called manufactured homes now? I could never remember.

"Where's Jade?" I asked Tammi.

"She went to the store. She thought you might like some real food since you've been down in Mexico all winter," she replied. "She'll be back shortly."

The tow-truck driver was right about a meal being not far from the motel. I was pretty sure he hadn't meant this place, but I wasn't about to quibble. "She's not wrong about that. I can't wait to get a taste."

I grinned. Tammi grinned back. We locked eyes and she made sure I saw hers flick the length of me. Mine followed, glued to her. I figured we were in some kind of a standoff, but what the hell. She wasn't shy either.

Women. I never could understand them at the best of times. This was shaping up to be one of those times.

Without Jade to distract me, I enjoyed a better look. For sure Tammi was no slouch in the assets department. She had a nice little body to go along with the pretty face. She was tall, too. Taller than me by a couple of inches. The extra length was all in her legs. More dark hair, but her eyes were the brightest blue. I'd have to watch out for this one, but I was more interested in finding out what Jade might offer up for dessert.

The door slammed and Jade revealed herself in a green sun dress. I knew right then and there I was going to have a problem, but not with Tammi. Jade was a plain-looking woman—not that it was a bad thing. Even so, the color of that dress set her up perfectly, and she knew it. She even went to the bother of applying a little lip gloss for makeup. Nothing else. It was all she needed.

I was hooked. And did she have legs. I scolded myself for thinking she might not beneath the jeans when I first laid eyes on her. The half I could see hanging down from the bottom of the dress looked interesting. It made me want to see the rest of them as soon as I could.

She smiled. "Were you wondering if I abandoned you?"

Just what I needed. Real trouble. "Only until Tammi told me where you were."

"Good. I don't like to be too predictable when I'm getting to know someone," she said.

It was looking like I might have a comfortable wait for my bike parts to show up.

Jade shooed us into the living room while she rattled dishes doing her thing in the kitchen. It was my chance to ask Tammi about her and I went for it. "What's Jade's story? She isn't a local. Did she end up getting stranded here too?"

"No. Well, yeah, kind of. Her boyfriend ended up down here. Jade wanted to support him, so she came with him. He was looking to keep his dream alive by escaping L.A. He wanted to live a life of leisure across the sea in that concrete jungle junk-yard with no money, no ideas, no hope, and no future."

"Junk-yard? What do you mean?" I heard similar stories so many times they all sounded the same. "And she's still here?"

"Slab City. It's on the east side of the sea. You probably haven't seen it."

The boy was busy enjoying the free lunch when the girl finally caught on and threw his lazy ass out. He skipped with her money, her car and her future. The dream died fast and my bet was this particular boy hasn't been seen in these parts since.

"How did that happen?" I wanted to know.

Tammi ignored the question and I knew my guess had to be as good as any. "She makes a little cash to get by. She found that wreck of a car over at Slab City. She had some help working on it. She got it running and when she drove by the motel there was a help wanted sign hanging in the window. You know the rest."

"Yes I do. And here I am." We shared the laugh at two of us stuck in this hell-hole and the fact that neither was getting out any time soon. Although, I'd bet good money that I'd be the first to leave.

"Hey, you two, you're having too much fun out there," Tammi called from the kitchen. "And stop talking about me. I'm only in the next room. I can hear everything."

I had one more question for Tammi. "You don't seem to mind it here. Did your adventures tire you out so much that you're home to stay too?"

I never did get an answer. Instead, Tammi excused herself to join Jade in the kitchen. I heard some whispering I couldn't make out, and then Tammi made a lame excuse about having to get home.

I didn't mind. I used the excuse to take the extra dishes off the table. I didn't want anything cluttering up the place besides me.

"There's candles in the drawer by the sink," she said.

I lit them while Jade put dinner on the table. In the subdued light everything looked pretty good. Especially Jade.

I might have thought about pinching myself. I didn't.

4

Long shadows advanced across the desert floor as the sun began slipping below the crest of the Santa Rosa mountains to the west. Cool darkness began exerting its hold over the hot desert day as the dark, hard night began overtaking the sunset.

"I'll turn on a light," I volunteered. I moved to get up. Jade shifted on the sofa and her dress came up, revealing a tanned thigh.

"Don't do that. Let's sit and watch the sun go down."

That was okay by me. I couldn't help grinning and she couldn't help smiling and then she stood up and turned to face me. She hiked up her dress just far enough to straddle me on the sofa.

"Damn you, woman. It's too dark for me to get a look," I told her.

"You'll see them."

I slipped cool hands beneath the loose material of her dress and fumbled until I felt fingertips on bare skin. I slowly ran my hands up the warmth of long, taut thighs. My hands slipped higher and I knew. Beneath the dress, Jade was naked. She sighed warm breath against my neck and relaxed into me.

Her lips moved against my ear. "You're still hungry, aren't you?" She pulled away and then her body pressed against mine. Her lips found my ear one more time and she exhaled.

If an alarm went off, I didn't hear it. I kept my eyes closed and listened, wide awake and tuned to what I could hear. Sheets rustled and a body moved, rewarding me. The mattress shifted. Jade was trying to sneak out of bed without disturbing me.

I cracked an eye to get a better look in the morning light streaming through a window. It definitely looked like a second helping would be in order. There'd be no leftovers if I had anything to do with it.

She turned toward me, not the least bit shy, and caught me looking. "If you want you can stay for a bit. I shouldn't be too long at work. It's not busy since the snowbirds started heading north. You can do the dishes and make the bed while you're waiting."

I smacked her rear and tried to pull her back down to the bed. She wasn't having any of it now that she had me where she wanted me. "I really have to go."

"So it's all right if I stay?" I asked. I wanted to be sure.

"Yes. I've never had a housekeeper before."

I brought my hand down fast, trying one more time to connect. She moved faster, dodging it. It connected with empty air.

"You'll have to do better than that. And in case you're wondering, you'll be having supper here again tonight."

I wouldn't say no to that.

5

It's known as **Slab** City, so called because all that's left are concrete slabs. The empty slabs, once occupied by Quonset huts and other buildings long torn down, are well beyond their best-before dates. Around a hundred desert rats populate the slabs that once were the foundations of an abandoned military barracks shut down and deserted in the early 60s.

Each slab comes with amenities: free camping and free parking. The only drawback: it's free of electricity and running water, too, but that doesn't appear to discourage anyone. New neighbors arrive in the late fall, when a small contingent of winter transients take over more of the slabs and provide some variety in the drab surroundings.

Where there are no rules, anything goes. Rusty junk inhabits more than a few of the slabs. There might be an old, broken-down bus or camper van or a trailer on top of some. On others, perhaps a tent. Some slabs are well kept. Most, not.

Mad Max would fit right in.

Street names on metal poles belie the condition of the place. Primrose Lane. Spa Road. Paradise Way. All roads going nowhere and getting there fast—just like the people camped out on the slabs.

The draw? Isolation. People of like mind. Escapees from the rat race. Drifters. Losers with nothing but an empty pack of cigarettes, a thirst for another sixer of beer, and a beater to drive to the store for more.

It's a perfect place where no one goes anywhere but down the closest road for beer and groceries and nothing else. Sometimes, they don't bother to come back.

And sometimes, they do.

6

Glass shattered. Something thumped in the living room. I wasn't close to wide awake when I opened my eyes and twisted out of bed in a hurry. With two feet firmly planted I looked around. I didn't recognize the bedroom. Groggy and confused, it hit me like a brick wall.

Right. Jade. If the woman was back from work, she had a hell of a way of announcing it. Then I remembered the beater and its squealing brakes. Maybe she drove it into the living room through no fault of her own.

My senses restored, I stood up from the edge of the bed. Whoever was making the noise, something said I was about to be in deep shit. Someone was trying to get in. Then I turned that around, and, based on the noise, figured someone was already in. The giveaway was the sound of glass crunching under someone's foot.

There was no about. I was in deep shit. In an instant I ran through the possibilities. Husband? Jade never said she was married. Boyfriend? Could be, and most likely. Whichever it was, she wouldn't be the first woman I slept with who had a husband or a boyfriend believed to be out of town.

It took another instant to finish with the guessing. I dropped down on all fours and reached under the bed. I crawled on my hands and knees to the closet. I checked behind the bedroom door. Finally. Naked and armed with a wooden baseball bat, I felt a lot better about walking into the living room. Thank you, Louisville.

Some dumbass was sprawled on a carpet of glass. He was struggling to get up onto his hands and knees. For a welcome change, the dumbass wasn't me. I cold-cocked him with a just-right tap of the bat. That put him back on his stomach in the broken glass.

More crunching glass behind me caused me to swing around. I faced Jade, who chose that moment to walk into the middle of it. I lowered the bat and let her know in no uncertain terms I wasn't happy. "Who the hell is the hockey player? Is there something you want to tell me?" I grabbed prince charming by the mullet and pulled his head up to give the woman a good look.

"What? No. He's not a hockey player. That's my ex."

No shit, Sherlock. I already had that figured out. To be certain, I asked. "Ex-husband"?

"No. He's my ex-boyfriend," she said.

I let go and boyfriend's head thumped down onto its broken-glass pillow. "Dammit, woman. Why the hell didn't you tell me he'd be coming back? I would have left this morning when you did."

"I didn't tell you because that asshole was already gone. He left town with my money, my car and his dreams. The useless bastard probably came back because he's broke. I don't want him here. We're done." She walked up and kicked him. Hard. "Did you hear that, you useless son of a bitch? You're not so brave now that you know there's a real man here, are you?"

Buddy groaned and she kicked him again. It was another good one. "Stop pretending and wake the hell up, you asshole. Get up, get out and don't come back. Ever. And where's my car?"

Buddy mumbled a mouthful of nothing.

"What?" Jade was almost screaming.

"Sold it," Buddy said through the shards of glass.

I presumed it wasn't what Jade wanted to hear.

"You son of a bitch!" Jade went at him again. This time, both feet flew, thumping against him one after the other as fast as she could go. By now I'd gathered enough sense to put on my shoes. I pulled her away and lifted her off the ground. She kept up with the kicking, feet flailing into empty air.

"Settle down. He's not worth it," I said, trying to calm her. I let her slip out of my arms. Her flailing feet touched down and took her in the direction of the man. It was as though a moth to a flame.

"Let Buddy get up so he can get on down the road and keep going."

Buddy got up on one foot and groaned getting all the way up on two. He swayed back and forth, as though unsure he should be leaving. He kind of took on a tilt in a couple of different directions, but he stayed on his feet, unsteady as they were. I wouldn't be too steady either if I'd just had a bat and a pair of boots work me over.

Jade picked up the bat and waved it. "If you ever

come back here you'll regret it. I'll see to that for sure."

She might be overdoing it, but could I blame her? It was pretty obvious she was angry, like maybe she'd waited for an opportunity like this for a while.

"All right. That's enough. Let him go," I said as I grabbed the bat away from the woman. Cut, bleeding and soon to be sore, Buddy limped toward the sliding door in the direction opposite to which he arrived. He tripped and stumbled through the broken door, heading for parts unknown and a long way from here.

Or so I hoped.

Jade behaved like she was unattached when she let me into her bed, and I guess she was. At least, that's what I believed. Apparently, nobody bothered to let good old Buddy in on the secret. Maybe his presence had something to do with that. He seemed to know his way around the place, and he certainly wasn't shy about crashing the party.

I wondered how long he and Jade had been together—not that it mattered. There was the possibility he might come back with a gun and a better idea of how to get in. If that turned out to be the case, I didn't want to be caught napping again.

After thinking about it, I decided Jade was awful quick to invite me into her home. Going by what happened with Buddy, it wasn't because she couldn't take care of herself. Her boots had put a pretty good dent in the man.

Someone owed me an explanation. Instead of patting myself on the back for my good fortune, I needed to keep my eyes and ears open. I didn't want to end up like Buddy crawling around in a pile of broken glass. Although, if last night was any sign, a man could get mighty comfortable with the woman and her bed.

Maybe I'd keep just one eye open.

I didn't like playing dumb. After fumbling in the kitchen and coming up with coffee, I tired of waiting for Jade to broach the subject. "Are you going to tell me about Buddy?"

"Buddy? Who the hell is Buddy? His name is Grant."

"That's what I said. Tell me all about Buddy. I want to know all about him. For my safety, not because I want to date him." It was the old *Keep enemies closer* thing.

Jade burst out laughing at the mix-up. "Don't make me do that. I'm sore all over. What did you do to me last night?"

"Only everything you asked me to. Now tell me more."

We broke out laughing again. This one had a sense of humor, at least. Even so, I had enough.

"You go take a bath," I told Jade. I'll clean up the glass in the living room. When you're done I'll cook something for you. You've got to keep your strength up now that you've got a man around to do the housecleaning."

Jade wagged a finger. "Don't you be trying to sweet-talk yourself back into my bed."

"If I recall, you're the one that invited me into it last night. And that's what giving me a look at your legs did for both of us."

"In that case, never again," she promised.

Promise or not, I slapped her ass. That was turning into a bad habit with this woman, but I couldn't resist. It looked so nice in those tight jeans. If I had my way, her ass would get slapped regularly.

Jade headed for the bathroom while I searched the fridge. We nattered back and forth until I finished sweating over a hot stove to fill her plate.

"That smells good and looks even better. I'm starving."

"Dig in, baby. It's all for you. I want to keep your strength up in case you have to go another round with Buddy."

"Yeah, you said something like that last night minus the Buddy reference. Look at me now."

I looked. "Damn, you're some woman."

"Does that mean you're coming back for more?" Jade wanted to know.

"I haven't left yet, have I? Now eat. We've got to keep your strength up."

She looked across the table at me. I sat and grinned like a high schooler. I couldn't think of anything to say. She said it for me.

"It's not my strength I'm worried about."

I let her eat while I wondered what might be coming my way next. Good old Buddy had to be missing his woman if what she had going with me was any guide.

Jade returned from the motel in short order. With few rooms to do, she was finished in an hour. The instant she was in the door, she took my hand and led me outside. "Come on, it's time."

"Hey now. I'm not some robot that you can command any time you want. I need time to rest and re-set."

"Oh, really? If I'm going to have a man like you around I'll need every bit of strength I can muster."

"Yeah, well, don't get too comfortable. I can always go back to my room at the motel."

"You could, but you still have to eat. My kitchen is connected to my bedroom," she said.

"And we both know what else is attached to your bedroom." I reached around and ran a hand beneath her dress. I gave her warm rear a firm squeeze and discovered she was commando.

"Come on, Frank, or we'll never get out of here."

"Don't be such a spoil sport." Reluctantly, I removed my hand. "You know the way to my heart."

"Yes I do. So far it seems to be legs and ass with only a bit of food now and again for good measure." Jade looked at me and smiled sweetly.

I **slipped a hand** beneath the sheets and made contact with a firm, warm thigh. I shook the woman attached to it and she sighed, not yet fully awake. "Are you planning on getting up for work, or are you going to play hooky?" Under the sheet, a single foot slid up and a knee rose, making a tent. It parted wide and I knew there wouldn't be any resistance. "I didn't think you were awake."

"I was pretending," Jade said. I was such a maniac the other night I didn't want you to think I should be arrested." The sheets rustled and she turned to look at me.

"You're preaching to the converted," I told her. "I already know you're a maniac. It's just a matter of figuring out to what degree and for how long you should be locked up." What the hell, I figured I should pay the rent somehow. "I'll make it all up to you by cooking breakfast."

"Breakfast? You're going to make breakfast?" Her legs came together almost as fast as they parted.

It led me to think good old Buddy wasn't much of a cook. "You know it." I jumped out of bed and took the easy way out. I already knew eggs and toast would cut it. In minutes Jade was at my side.

"Something smells good out here."

"Yeah, and now it looks good out here."

Jade hugged me before sitting down to devour everything I put on the plate, but that was all right. Hungry women appealed to me. "You eat like a death row inmate devouring a last meal."

"I wouldn't put it quite that way, but it seems to me a woman had better keep her strength up when she has a man like you around."

"That's what I'm afraid of."

She looked at me, serious, all of a sudden. "I know you're not going to be around for long. Even so, there's no sense sleeping at my place and keeping a room at the motel. If you want, you can bring your things here."

Jade didn't use the *move-in* words. I was happy. "Are you sure? I don't want to cramp your style. I could be a serial sex maniac on the prowl for someone just like you." She couldn't help grinning and I knew right away that's what we were both hoping for.

"In that case, you got lucky, baby. You found me," she smiled.

"Your friend Buddy isn't going to take exception, is he? He could always come back," I worried.

"He won't be back now that he knows you're here."

That's what I figured, too. In fact, I wondered if that's the reason I got the invite in the first place. "Let's hope not."

Jade gave her dress a flip, giving me a show of never-ending leg as she went out the door. Like a dog in heat,

I chased after her.

"Are you planning on following me to work, too?"

"Not at all. I wanted to see if the sun would shine through that dress enough to give me a look at what it's covering up."

"If you're good, you'll get a look when I get back," she promised.

"In that case, don't be too long." I started thinking I'd be liking it here.

A lot.

I stood back and surveyed the damage Buddy did during the break-in. A fix for the sliding door in Jade's living room would require a permanent repair.

I tripped over a stash of tools and discovered a saw in a box in the front porch. I cut a sheet of thin plywood to fit and screw-nailed it in place. I slid the door open and closed in its track. It was heavy, but it worked.

As though on cue, Jade appeared. "You weren't at work for long." She looked pretty good in that dress.

"I only had a couple of rooms to do. I checked you out of the motel. We'll take the car and get your stuff later. Was the door hard to fix?"

"I found some tools. Am I going to get paid?"

She smiled. I always figured if a man could keep a woman smiling it was a good thing.

"No, baby, you're gonna get laid."

I was right about that. "What's the difference?"

She laughed. I never liked it when that happened.

"I guess that's why I have the job and you're the broke-ass biker from down Mexico way."

I smacked her ass. I needed to stop doing that, even if this time she deserved it.

"Watch it, fella," she warned me, smiling.

"I am watching it. In fact, I've been watching it since the first time I saw it."

"Speaking of getting paid, Dell gave me this." She handed me an envelope with my room refund. "There's no parcel for you yet."

"You're changing the subject again." I looked at her, not saying anything. "You look pretty."

Jade blushed. She wasn't expecting a compliment. "What a nice thing to say. Thank you."

In light of my mechanical problem, I was happy to be here. Things would be a lot worse had it happened south of the border. I had a place to stay that wasn't going to cost much more than a little food and some sleep. I wanted to celebrate. What better way to do it than with a pretty girl hanging out beside me, even if there was no one to see us? "How about we take a walk so I can show you off?" I'd be able to slip in an errant squeeze to add to the tension between us.

"In that case, we'll walk down to the fingers," Jade said.

"The fingers? What do you mean?" I wanted to know.

"Back in the 60s this was the place to be. Every one of those man-made docks built out into the Sea had rows of RVs and trailers sitting on them," she explained. "They were named for Naples, Venice, Acapulco, Honolulu. The bigger ones to the north had mobile homes. They called them all fingers. You'll see when we get there."

"This place must have been party central back in the

drug-addled 50s," I said.

"A lot of them were older, but they brought their families out with them. There were powerboat races, fish derbies, that kind of stuff. Then rainstorms and a couple of hurricanes blew through. The runoff raised the level of the sea and the hurricanes swept clean what was left of the place."

"How long did the good-times last?"

"It lasted until the mid-70s. If you look around and you can see what didn't get flooded out or blown away. Deserted resort towns are scattered up and down both sides of the sea. They're all trying to cling to the past."

So that's what they were. "On my way north I rode through what's left of a town to take a look. I thought it looked like real estate development tracts. So much went into building all of it—the people, the homes, the businesses. I can't believe in just a few years it was blown away."

"Sometimes I feel like I'm living in a ghost town, and I guess I am. Then you showed up and I forgot all about it. I'm glad you're here."

My walk with Jade confirmed it. Bombay Shores was a ghost town. It had nothing going for it. "What do you say we keep on walking to the motel? I need to get my ride to your place."

I found Dell in the motel office. He was busy manhandling the mail. "I figured you'd be in today. And no, no parts yet. I'll be sure to let you know."

That was disappointing news, but it was still early.

"Did you get your refund?" he wanted to know.

"You bet. Thanks for letting me back out of the deal

we had. I didn't know I'd end up finding a place to stay."

"I know. Watch out for that one. She's a sly little thing."

Was Dell warning me? "How so?"

"I'll let you figure that out for yourself."

I hesitated for a minute, wanting to ask Dell more questions. Instead, I made for my ride. I tied my bag on and lifted the bagger off of its kick-stand.

"That's heavy. What do you want me to do?" Jade asked.

"I tried giving you some direction the other night, but you went off on your own."

"Well no wonder," she exclaimed. "You overwhelmed me and I was speechless."

"Just because you couldn't talk doesn't mean you were speechless. No kissing up until we're home. Now get behind and push to help me get started."

"Isn't that what I told you to do?"

"Smartypants."

"I'm not wearing pants," she said.

"Damn you, woman, don't tell me that now."

"I was hoping we'd get home faster if you knew."

"Bitch."

"You love it."

"Yes, I do—especially when the bitch isn't wearing panties. Now come on. Let's get a move-on. If you're lucky I'll still have some energy left when we get to where I'm going."

I pushed my ride to her trailer, and she waited while I eased the bike onto its side-stand. She rushed inside ahead of me, leaving the door open. I walked in where a sight for my tired eyes forced them wide open. Jade's dress was up over her hips and she was bent over the table, resting on her elbows.

I didn't need to be asked twice with a view like that staring me in the face. I dropped trou and went at her like a madman. She reached under to give me a helping hand. When it was over, she didn't even blink.

Neither did I.

"Tammi is coming over tonight. Is that all right?" She pushed off the table and pulled her dress down over her bare ass.

"Of course. I like her. She's good company."

I wanted to know more about Jade after Dell's comment at the motel. Had I not broke down, I wouldn't be here. That, and running into Jade at the motel was chance, too. Neither of us could have figured on meeting up with the other. There was no doubt that all of it was accidental.

Still, I was welcomed into Jade's bed pretty quick. And maybe she was being a little too sweet, but the hair on the back of my neck wasn't even close to standing up. From what I could see, there weren't many prospects around a ghost town for a woman on the prowl for some strange.

There was something nagging at me, though, and that was Buddy's visit. It was obvious he wasn't expecting to find me here. What was he doing trying to break in? Was he looking for something?

If he was, what was it?

8

I answered the knock at the door and opened it to greet Tammi. "The girl is busy cooking. She pretends to be a kitchen princess when she's not being a bed bunny."

I laughed with Tammi.

Jade couldn't resist a comeback. "I heard that. If you want to eat dinner, you better start kissing butt," she advised me.

"I was doing some of that a little earlier, remember? You were asking for it then, too."

Tammi smacked her rear on the way by. "How about it, sailor? I hear you've got stamina for two."

"You'll have to get me drunk first." I'd have stamina for three if Jade would let Tammi join us. She was hot.

"What are we drinking, Jade?" she asked.

"And I don't drink," I said.

"Too bad," Tammi said with a grin.

I called into the kitchen. "Tammi's making a pass at me."

"Don't feel special, Frank. If she caught you, she wouldn't know what to do."

I wasn't so sure about that, but I put the thought on the back burner. If ever there was a chance to find out more about Jade, this was it. While cooking duties kept the woman busy in the kitchen, I led Tammi into the living room. "You can start by telling me all you know about our little kitchen princess. If you don't, I'll spank you right here."

"How about we do both?" Tammi's grin was wide.

"Jade might object. Are you gonna talk or not?"

"I don't know much beyond what I told you the other day. Jade showed up looking for a job. She was over at Slab City before that. The rumor mill said she was shacked up with a guy from Calexico. Or maybe it was L.A."

Calexico? L.A.? Which was it? I said nothing and allowed her to go on.

"Apparently Grant screwed off with all of her money and her car after a supposed drug deal went sour. He probably had people looking for him because of that, thus the reason he ran off. You'll have to ask Jade for anything more than that, because that's all I know."

If that was Jade's story according to Tammi, it was a short one. "Do you think Jade could have been involved in the drug deal?"

Tammi hesitated before answering. "I don't think so, but anything is possible, I guess."

"Did she mention I had a visit from Buddy?"

"Buddy? That's a good one. He was here? She never mentioned it."

I wondered why.

"That's his work on the door. Or rather, it's my repair job. Buddy tried to get in the other morning while I was sleeping."

"How far did he get?" Tammi wanted to know.

"As far as on his hands and knees on the living room floor. He ended up swimming on his belly in broken glass after I cold-cocked him with the baseball bat I found in the bedroom."

"Well, at least now he knows you're here. He probably won't come back."

"I haven't told you the best part yet." Tammi was all ears. "Our little kitchen princess kicked the shit out of Buddy when he was down."

"No way. Jade," she called to her. "Was that your ex from Slab City?"

"Yeah. It was Grant. I can't seem to get rid of that son of a bitch. I hope he got the idea when he was introduced to Frank."

"Why are you calling him Buddy?" Tammi asked.

"Because that's the name I gave him."

"You're nuts," she said, before reaching around to grab my ass. "Don't be telling her mine, either."

Jade chose that instant to come into the living room. "Come on, you two. No more groping. Sit your asses down and dig in."

I gestured in Jade's direction. "See what I mean? Kitchen princess."

"Yeah and you won't be seeing the bedroom bunny again if you're not careful," she warned.

"Be nice, Frank. I think she might mean it," Tammi said.

"Nah. I'll sweet-talk her just like I did the other

night." I winked at Tammi.

"As I recall, you weren't doing much talking, Frank."

"Yeah, baby, and when you were trying to talk, you weren't making any sense."

Tammi's eyes lit up. "Oh, do tell me more. Please."

"Later, tater," Tammi said. "When the man's asleep."

Jade rattled drawers and slammed doors in her attempt to make sure I was wide awake by the time she pulled at the covers. She was successful, and I rolled over and looked up at her while propping my head on a bent elbow.

"I think Tammi has a crush on you."

She was right, but I was smart enough to know I'd be damned to eternal hellfire if I admitted it. "It's not a crush when all she wants to do is get laid. Stop telling her about what we've been doing. What if she shows up here when you're at work? Would you like me to take care of her, too?"

"The way she's been talking, I don't think it would take much for her to do that."

"You didn't say no, baby." I was testing the waters.

"That's because I'm not going to leave you with anything to take care of her with."

Oh-oh. The consequences weren't looking so good. "So then, you're going to cut off my balls?"

"No, that's not exactly what I had in mind for your balls. Why don't I show you instead?"

I shared breakfast with Jade and patted her on the ass before sending her off to work. I didn't want to be surprised a second time by someone interrupting my beauty sleep first thing in the morning. I stayed up and killed time by unpacking. I put a few things away in an open drawer Jade had emptied for me. I nosed through a couple of the others and got bored when I didn't come up with anything more interesting than bras and panties.

The rest of my stuff I hung in the closet beside some of her dresses. I took a quick look at jackets and nightgowns. I knew I'd probably never see her in one of those.

My attention turned to the boxes on the floor. Shoes, most likely. I bent down for a better look just because I could. Shoe boxes. I opened a couple. No surprises. I picked up the last shoe box and hefted it. It was heavier than the rest. Boots, probably.

I set the box back down. It was too small to be a boot box. I picked it up again. It slipped out of my hand and landed on the floor. The top flew off. I jumped back, lost my balance, and banged my head against the door frame.

9

I took a step back. Rubbed at the growing bump on my head. The contents of the box were lying on the floor. Green plastic covered it. Definitely not shoes, in my experience. Possibilities raced through my thoughts.

I bent down for a better look. Turned the bag over. There was a sticker on the plastic. A black scorpion sticker. The hair on the back of my neck finally caught up and stood straight up. Why would a scorpion—

Just when I started to think I'd be okay here. I began pacing back and forth in the bedroom before sitting on the bed.

It had to be coke. The quantity wasn't small, either. I figured about five keys. I hefted the bag. Roughly ten pounds. And it wasn't just any coca. The package was marked with a scorpion. That meant Colombian. Baja. Tijuana. Mexicali was 70 miles south, just down the road. Those guys ran down the Baja and across to Sonora on the mainland.

I sat on the bed, leaned over, and put my head in my

hands—like it would do any good. The realization finally hit home. I was shacked up with a woman holding cartel drugs. A lot of cartel drugs. Another light-bulb went off. It suddenly became clear why Jade's legs had parted so easily. That's why she was so happy to have me between them. And that's why she told me I could stay with her while I waited out my bike parts.

Jade needed a watchdog in case the boyfriend returned for the goods. Any dog would have done, but I was the one that showed up and made it obvious I was sniffing around. It was all coming together.

Buddy's visit wasn't an accident. He came looking for something, and I just discovered what it was. He wanted the coca. No wonder her ex was trying to get into the place. He had a huge monkey on his back, one that would get him killed if those drugs didn't get back to their rightful owner.

Because why would some chapulíno, some grasshopper—a small scale street dealer—have five keys of coca in her closet? That was no small quantity of drugs for someone to be selling on the street. That amount would get a man killed in a hurry when the wrong people found out.

Did Jade have any idea about the trouble she was holding in her closet? Who was the owner? Jade? Had she stashed the drugs for safekeeping? Perhaps Buddy knew they were there and wanted to add her drugs to his collection. According to Jade, he already had her car and all of her money.

Sure as shit Jade would know the closet was a bad place to store dope. That must have been why she wanted me around. The place would look occupied while she went off to work. There was one problem. Where would a woman like Jade, making beds in a two-bit ghost-town motel, get money to lay down for five keys of coca?

Sure as shit she didn't own it. If it wasn't her coke, and it wasn't Buddy's, whoever owned it would come knocking on the door pretty damned quick once they found out where the coke was stashed.

No way did I want to be around when that happened.

Did Tammi know? She spent a lot of time hanging out with her friend. The woman needed to know what was going on if she was going to keep putting herself in the hot-seat with Jade. It was time to talk to her.

I took a chance Tammi would be home and headed across the street. I wanted to kick down the door and knocked instead. The sight of the woman in cutoffs and a tight white tee made for a welcome distraction. She arched her back and leaned against the door frame with her hands behind her, forcing me to push past to get in. Her breasts were definitely firm. So were the nipples poking out from beneath the white shirt.

"I just made a fresh pot. You want some coffee?" she asked with a smile.

"That'd be great." I sat down at the table and looked around. Her kitchen was neat. Tidy. Organized. She poured a mug and slid it across the table before sitting down opposite me.

"So what are you doing here, Frank?" Tammi asked. "You're obviously well taken care of. You're not tired of what you have across the street already, are you? What's up?"

This one was no dummy, but not for the reason she

thought. "I'm swearing you to secrecy. Promise me you won't say a word to anyone about what I'm going to tell you."

"Have you killed someone?" She waited, and I figured she was only half joking.

"Not yet."

"Then go ahead. Talk," she insisted.

I took a breath before going on. "Jade told me yesterday I could stay with her until I got back on the road. She emptied a drawer for me in the bedroom. This morning after she left I figured what the hell, I might as well put some of my stuff away in the closet."

If I was smart, I would have left it at that. I've never been smart when it comes to the women in my life. "When I was done I got curious, so I looked through some of her things. You know what men are like."

Tammi nodded. She knew what men were like, all right.

My eyes wandered to a hint of perfect breasts on display beneath the thin shirt. Satisfied, they roamed back up. She waited until my eyes met hers. "Take your time. I don't mind. So What did you find, a dildo bigger than your dick?"

I snorted in disbelief. "What the hell has that woman been telling you about me?"

"Telling me? She's been bragging about you since she climbed off of you that first night, and I'm not talking about your sweet disposition. You want to know what else?"

The answer was coming whether I asked for it or not.

"I've been putting myself to sleep daydreaming about you ever since." Tammi's face went pink. Hell, I think mine did, too. "Remind me why you came over here again." Her eyes bored into mine, unblinking, waiting.

"It's about Jade. She's holding Colombian coke. In her closet, of all places. I figure about five keys worth, maybe more."

It took Tammi a moment to comprehend, and then she looked away, like she was registering what I said and was trying to come up with a response. She cleared her throat and hesitated again before raising her eyes to meet mine. "Are you serious? Could it belong to her ex?" Tammi's eyes shifted away from mine again.

"It's looking to me like Buddy was left holding the empty bag. I'm thinking the only reason I'm here is because she needs someone to be a watchdog when she's at work."

"Jade couldn't have known she'd meet up with you," Tammi said. "You're only here because your ride broke down."

"Yeah, that was bad luck all right. I broke down when I went to pull out of the casino. I needed a place to stay and the flatbed driver told me about the motel."

"You were at the casino first? How did I manage to miss you?" The smile she flashed looked insincere.

"I spied the flatbed in the lot. I waited outside for the driver to crawl out of whatever rock he was under. I needed the tow and a place to stay. He told me about the Palms."

"It's the only place close by."

"Shit. What the hell am I going to do about Jade? I'll wake up in her bed and find a Mexican sicario leaning over to put a bullet in the back of my head when I'm not paying attention. Wide awake or asleep, it won't matter. And I won't be the only one growing stiff and cold. Jade will be bleeding out beside me."

"I'll take you in if you want. I don't need a man to protect any drugs," she assured me. She avoided looking at me.

"I couldn't move in with you. You and Jade would be at it tooth and nail. I don't want that for either of you."

"You're too sweet. Have you heard anything about your bike parts?"

"I called a friend. He said he already shipped them to the motel. I expect they'll be showing up shortly."

Tammi directed her gaze at me. I could see wheels were definitely turning.

"I won't be so sweet when you hear this. That five keys is worth around forty thousand dollars per. Don't ask how I know. If she can get it north to a major city like Chicago or New York, it's worth even more."

I had to let her know she wasn't safe. "Nobody, but nobody, is going to let missing drugs with values like that stay missing for long. Especially a cartel. When someone finds out about the drugs in Jade's closet, the cell-phone towers will be burning up. An SUV filled with sicarios won't be far away."

"What are you going to do?"

"I'm thinking about blowing town. The sooner the better."

Tammi stood up and paced, making her look concerned. She looked like I knew too much. She didn't look like she wanted to skip town. "This is news to me. I need some time to digest it. Now get out of here before Jade gets home and sees you walking across the street."

"Are you coming over for dinner later?" I wanted to know. "We should make it look like another normal meal, don't you think?"

"Do you think I should, Frank?"

"I'd like it if you did."

Even if the sicarios were on their way, I still wanted someone around I could trust.

10

Jade dropped the heavy package on the table. It landed with a thud and I knew right off what it was. Her long face telegraphed she would finally get rid of her freeloader. Considering I was her makeshift burglar alarm, it was no wonder.

No matter. I was ready to hit the road once I did the work to get my ride fixed. I'd be good to go and I wasn't about wasting time. "I'll be out working on the bike," I said, as I picked up the carton and headed out to my bagger. Hitting the road couldn't come soon enough.

A disappointed Jade walked past me. "I'll take Tammi and pick up some groceries. Is there anything special you'd like?"

Yeah, see if you can pick up a handgun for me at the liquor store. Or maybe you've got one stashed in the closet. In that case, I'd like to borrow it.

"No, I'm good. I'll see you when you get back. Is Tammi coming over?" Misery always loved company. Especially my misery.

"I'll ask her."

I had the clutch installed and was busy buttoning up the primary by the time the women showed. Jade hugged me. I looked over Jade's shoulder at Tammi. She turned away, unable to bring herself to look at me.

"Hey now, what's with you two?" The women were looking good.

"Nothing, why?"

"Look at the both of you." I held Jade at arm's length. It occurred to me it was where I should have kept her from the start.

"What? What are you talking about?"

"My two favorite women are all dressed up with nowhere to go."

Jade grinned. Tammi's face turned red. I knew why. "I dug this out of my closet. It's nothing special," Tammi said.

"Did you tell Tammi how much I like seeing a good-looking woman in a dress?" I asked Jade.

Tammi blushed again, and I figured I'd better shut the hell up. Women. Sometimes they can be so obvious. More often than not, a man can be so stupid that he ends up in the same place as a woman with five keys of cartel coke and doesn't know when to leave.

I changed the subject in a hurry. "What did you pick up for dinner?"

"There's steaks and potatoes for baking."

"In that case I'll fire up the barbecue." I walked by Tammi past the plywood door.

"I'll help you," she said.

I was glad for Tammi's company. Jade couldn't resist a comment from the kitchen. "Don't you be grabbing his ass."

"I won't, I promise." Then she whispered. "I want

more than his ass now."

"Stop being a tease and help me put the steaks on. Screw the potatoes. I'm in no mood. I'll nuke them."

Tammi grabbed my arm. "What happened? Why are you upset? Did Buddy come back again?" She squeezed just hard enough to let me know she was there.

"It's those damned drugs. I haven't stopped looking over my shoulder since I found them in the closet."

"What are you going to do?" she wanted to know

"I don't know. If Buddy gets anywhere near this place again, I'm pretty sure I'll end up stuffing the drugs up his ass. For good measure, I'll send him packing toward the border."

"And Jade?"

I didn't know what to tell her.

"You've only been here a few days, Frank, but I can tell you like her a lot."

"That five key bundle of coca in Jade's closet is a deal-breaker. I could end up in prison if someone makes the wrong call. And if they make the right call, I could end up full of lead. You could too if the people taking that call show up when you're here."

My options weren't looking good.

"Now you've got me worried.

"You should be. I know I am. My life isn't worth the money those five keys of coca is worth to the people that own it. Neither is yours."

Tammi's hand brushed against mine. I grabbed it and squeezed.

"What are you two whispering about out here? Shit, Frank, you've got the steaks on already. The potatoes aren't even started."

"I'll nuke them."

Jade could tell something was bothering me. Tammi got smart and left us alone. "What's with you?"

"Well, for starters, you've got five kilos of Colombian in your closet."

Tammi gave me a dirty look. "What were you doing in my closet?"

"You told me I could stay with you. Remember the empty drawer you said I could have? When I was putting some of my things away I kicked over a box. Surprise, it wasn't shoes."

"How do you know it's Colombian?"

Did she even know? "The scorpion is a dead giveaway. Mexicali is 70 freaking miles distant. That's like next door. Do the cartels ring any bells for you? And what about Buddy? He was here looking for something, wasn't he?" I was angry now that I knew I was taken in by her. "Now I know what it was."

The anger in my voice brought Tammi back to the patio. She must have thought we were close to coming to blows. "It's bad enough you got me into this thing with that asshole Buddy, but you got Tammi into it, too."

"You told her? What the hell have you two been doing while I'm at work?" She looked at Tammi, eyes ablaze, and then back at me, waiting.

"I went to Tammi's to see if she knew what the hell was going on. Guess what? She didn't. She's over here visiting you almost every night. If she happens to be here when the shit hits the fan, she'll end up dead beside you."

"You're exaggerating, Frank."

But I wasn't. Even if she wouldn't accept it, I knew

I was right. "Tammi, you've got to get out of here. Now. I'm sorry. I'll bring your dinner over when it's done, okay?"

Tammi's face went pale. She didn't say a word. She looked at me and nodded and left to walk across the street. We were alone.

"As for you—" I began.

11

It was dark when I crossed the street with Tammi's steak. I knocked and waited for what seemed like forever. "Come on, open the door. I brought your steak—" I called through her door.

Tammi pushed the door wide and greeted me with a huge grin. She was out of her dress and back to cutoffs. "I was just changing. Give me a second."

She permitted me a good look before she finished pulling the t-shirt all the way down over her breasts. "How can you be so dumb? I was dressed for you tonight. Couldn't you even figure that out? What's the point of looking nice and not have you notice?"

For sure I was noticing now. "I'm sorry. I noticed that you changed." I noticed her naked breasts, too, and the dark nipples that tipped them.

"Small comfort," she let me know.

"More comfort if you go put the dress back on. How about it?" I couldn't help grinning. In return, she gave me that look a woman gets when a man does something stupid. She quickly changed it into a smile. "What are you grinning at?"

"Well, I'm thinking if you put the dress on, I've got you. And if you do, you've got me. I'd call that a Mexican standoff," I had to admit.

"In that case, don't go away."

Why does it take a woman a lifetime to throw on a dress? I nuked the potato and set the table.

"Here I am."

"So that's why it took so long. Que chula niña." She couldn't help blushing. I continued to stare at her.

"You like?" She did a pirouette.

"Si. De nuevo por favor. Again please."

Tammi looked pleased as punch. She grinned and wrapped her arms around me. Man that I was, the drugs I discovered across the street put me in such a fix that I never considered letting my hands wander. "Okay, enough. Eat, woman."

She sat at the table. I sat across from her.

"Have you decided what we're going to do about Jade?"

We? Where the hell did that come from?

"I don't know. I put my ride together this afternoon. It's good to go."

"Does that mean that you are, too?" she wanted to know.

"Well—" I hesitated.

"You can say it."

"Yes. I'm good to go, too."

"Alone?"

I didn't have a ready answer. There might be an outside chance Jade didn't know the true value of what was stashed in her closet. My best guess was she did. If that was the case, she wouldn't be going anywhere with the likes of me.

"I'm not going with Jade, that's for sure. I don't need her complications in my life. She's sitting on five kilos of coke. She won't be looking to go anywhere with a broke-ass biker. And I don't think she's hanging onto the coke to stuff it up her nose."

"You think she wants to sell it." It wasn't a question.

"She probably put some feelers out. That's not too smart, considering the quantity and who owns it. Sure as shit, there's going to be something coming down the pipe. It's only a matter of time. I don't want to be here when time runs out.

"Is there anything I can do?"

"I don't know. Have you got a bag?" I had to get Tammi out of here. If she showed up at Tammi's when shit was going down, she'd end up dead right beside Jade.

"I'll be right back." Tami returned with a backpack. A battered helmet hung off the side. Judging by the thump the backpack made when it hit the floor, it was already packed.

"I've got a couple of dresses. Two shirts and a pair of jeans. A pair of heels. Three panties, three g-strings and short-shorts. A tube top and tampons. Will I need anything else?"

I gave her the manly man look. "I don't know. Where are you going? And why are you bringing all that underwear?" I grinned so hard I thought my face would break.

She ignored me. It's funny how a woman will do that to a man sometimes. Instead, she started haranguing me.

"Let's see if I have this right. You've been shacked up for days with a woman you ran into in a parking lot—literally. She's spreading her legs like there's no tomorrow and grinning like the cat that ate the canary. You tripped over five keys of Colombian in her closet. Her ex is looking to score and somehow, I don't think he wants to get laid."

I couldn't argue with that. It was all true. She wasn't finished, though.

"There's a reason Buddy hasn't forgotten about that coke. It probably has something to do with cartel drugs, wouldn't you think? All that, and you want to stay a few more days with someone because she has a tight little you-know-what? Frank, get real, man."

I didn't have to think about anything she said. It made too much sense. "Look, I never said I was a rocket scientist when it comes to women. And by the way, you need to stop spending time at Jade's if you don't want to get caught up in this."

She looked at me like I was crazy. Probably with good reason. "For crying out loud, give your head a shake. Both of them. If you haven't figured out what you should do next, I'll be happy to do it for you."

Okay, so the jury was in. I was crazy.

"Get back on the trail you rode in on. Backtrack. Turn right onto the 86. Can I make it any plainer?"

"Well, since you put it that way—" I couldn't say she was wrong.

"It's time, Frank. You know what Jade is up to. Get yourself out of a situation that could be fatal."

She was telling me what I was only thinking up to

now. "Shit, we're in this together. We both need to get out. The sooner the better." It was that simple. "I'll wait until Jade falls asleep. I'll push my bike over to your place, just in case. That'll give us an out if the shit hits the fan while we're still here."

I said *if*, but it was more likely *when*.

"That sounds good to me."

"There's one more thing." I had to tell her.

"What did you leave out?"

"Jade's got a juguete in the closet with the dope."

"What are you talking about?" Tammi was pissed now.

"A juguete. Sorry. I've been in Mexico too long. It's slang for a gun."

"So she means business."

"That's what I figured too. I didn't want to tell you because I didn't want to keep you up."

"It's too late for that. I've been up nights since I first laid eyes on you."

That again. "I'm going back to Jade's."

Tammi started to say something. I didn't want to listen to another word. I put a finger to her lips and hugged her. This time, I reached around with a hand and squeezed. Her ass was firm enough to take my mind off my troubles, that's for sure. She sighed as her body molded itself to mine.

"You better go before she gets suspicious. If you don't, I'm going to take off this dress and let you look at more than my breasts."

She was right. Reluctantly, I headed back across the street, anxious to get packed. I'd wait for Jade to fall asleep, pack my bag and be out the door, home-free and gone. I'd be sneaking away in the night like the dog I was. I wouldn't be taking any prisoners. If Tammi wanted to throw a leg over and come along for the ride, that would be fine by me.

If she didn't, there'd be no turning back for stragglers.

12

I wasn't in a hurry to get across the street and back to Jade's place. I knew what I had to do, though. It was a matter of how to get it done. If I could keep Jade from asking questions, I wouldn't have a problem. If she became suspicious, well, I'd have to handle that road when it came time.

She met me at the door. "How did Tammi like the steak?"

"Cooked to perfection, just the way she likes it."

"I'll bet. What else did she like?"

What I didn't like was the bitter sound in Jade's voice and the icy stare she was handing out. "Nothing. I'm here now, aren't I? And while I'm here, I have a question for you."

"What's that?"

"What's your plan for the coke in your closet? Have you got a buyer?"

"Why? Is the broke-ass biker going to make me an offer?"

Jade's voice had a hard edge to it. Tough. I

wondered how tough she'd be when the shit hit the fan and cartel sicarios were breaking down the door.

"Even if I was interested I wouldn't make any offers. Instead, I'd have disappeared down the road the first time I laid eyes on it sitting in your closet." What the hell would I do with five keys of cartel coca? I had about as much of an idea as she did by the look of it.

"Whatever you say."

"More than likely you'd be sitting here empty-handed, trying to scream past a gun barrel stuffed down your throat by a cartel hit man. It wouldn't even be their best hit man. When he finally figured out you didn't know where the dope was, you'd end up with two bullets in the back of your head for the trouble you knew."

"Stop talking, Frank. You've said enough."

"What's the gun in the closet for? Are you trying to be the town toughie too?"

"What the hell do you think it's for? I need the protection."

"If the dope doesn't get you killed, that gun will. Do you think those guys are amateurs screwing around like you are? A woman with a gun is mincemeat to a cartel SUV filled with killers. What the hell are you doing? Do you even know? Coke in the closet? What the hell is that about?"

"Frank, let it go."

"It's not the five keys they care about so much. It's all about the message the missing five keys sends out. Nobody screws with their drugs. Ever. But besides that, you've got street value close to a couple of hundred-thousand dollars wasting away in your closet."

She shook her head. "Enough. I'm going to bed. Are you coming?"

"I'm going to take a shower."

"You better not be washing her stink off."

"You want to smell me first?"

I dried off and showed up in the bedroom expecting cold shoulder and another argument. Instead, she pulled the sheet back to reveal a naked body and legs already spread.

"Come here, baby. Make me feel good," she said.

I might be able to make her feel good, but I wasn't feeling so good about it.

I put Jade to sleep the only way I knew how. I waited for her breathing to even out before climbing out of bed. I dressed and headed outside to walk my ride to the street. I pushed it past Tammi's and down an alley toward the highway.

In the back of my head, I knew I shouldn't go back for my bag. Hell, I could buy new once I got a job and some money. And then I realized that might be a while. I went back to collect my belongings.

In the dark I tip-toed to the bedroom. I waited in the open door and listened to Jade's breathing. It was even and slow. I made for the closet and slid the door open. Images of the open road I'd be riding on in mere minutes flashed through my head. The hard click of a hammer being pulled back woke me out of my reverie. I froze.

I didn't have to guess where she had the muzzle pointed. I might not be so lucky getting my ass out of Jade's place after all. My brain went into useless overdrive. My plan wasn't going so well. Cold sweat started its run down my back.

I should have taken Dell's hint and stayed at the Palms. I should have stayed with Tammi and let her take her dress off. I should have looked the other way when I caught sight of Jade's car bumping into the motel parking lot. I should have convinced myself her ass looked fat in those jeans with the flaps over the back pockets.

Like any of it would have made a difference. It was too late now. I only wanted one thing. I wanted to get my unlucky ass out of here alive and back on the road in one piece. I played it for sympathy. I was quaking in my boots.

"Are you going to shoot me in the back?" I had no doubt she would if she thought I was trying to steal the drugs.

"What are you looking for?" Her voice was hard again.

"Only for what I brought to the picnic." I should have been smart enough to leave it behind. The little I had wasn't worth shit anyway. Why did I think jeans and t-shirts were so valuable that I had to come back for them?

"Toss your bag over here."

I half-ass turned and threw the bag. Tammi used one hand to rifle through it while she kept the pistol aimed. She finished and threw it at my feet. "Get out."

I didn't waste time. I got out.

I don't know why I looked both ways before crossing the dark, dead street in the dead town on the dead sea, but I was glad I did. The SUV was parked in plain view on the deserted street under a burned-out street lamp. Jade's luck was about to run out in a hurry. No way did I want to be around for that. I opened Tammi's door and walked into the dark trailer. I couldn't see a thing. A hand reached out and pulled me close. Warm lips moved against my ear.

"Well?" She bathed me in body heat and warm breath. I could feel every inch of her.

"She pulled a gun. I didn't think I was getting out of there alive."

"And that surprised you?" Tammi asked.

"Yes. No. Not any more." Funny how I couldn't make up my mind.

"Well?"

Again with the well. "You're not going to cut me any slack, are you?"

"No. I'm not."

"We barely know each other." It was true.

"Yes, but there's a plus to that," Tammi said.

"What is it?" I wanted to know.

"We didn't meet in a parking lot. We were actually introduced."

I grinned in the dark. "True."

"I don't need you to babysit any drugs."

That was a definite plus. "And that's good. But Tammi, I'm busted flat and we're not even in Baton Rouge yet. I barely have enough money to make my way home."

"I cleaned out my stash. I have a little traveling money I managed to save. Oh, and there's two more little details you need to know."

"Only two?"

"I threw in another dress."

She had been listening after all.

"And I was a dancer for a year before I moved back here."

So I was right. "Come on. We have to get out of here. The back way. There's an SUV down the street and I'm thinking whoever is inside hasn't come to take the guided tour of the fingers."

"I wonder if her ex gave her up?"

"Him or someone else, Jade is in for a world of hurt. Come on, we have to go." Together we quick-stepped out the back and down the alley.

"Should we warn her?" Tammi asked.

"She was using me. I have no idea what she was doing with you. Maybe she was using you, too. If you want to go back, we'll go together, but you better know what you'll be in for. It won't be anything like you see in a movie."

An engine raced. There was a crash. Tin bent and was crushed. I halted and found an opening to allow me to see Jade's pace. The SUV was sticking out of where the living room should be. That put me in hurry-up mode. Even so, like passing a freeway wreck, I had to look. Light from the SUV's open doors outlined two shadows moving toward the house. Tammi came up beside me.

"You still want to go back?"

A man disappeared into the trailer. In seconds, two gunshots boomed down the empty street. A double tap, the sound unrestrained by any houses in the deserted ghost town.

"Come on, we need to get this show on the road." I huffed and puffed on the run to the bike. The Sol and tortillas down in Mexico had done a job. "I'm getting too old for this, woman."

"You're not too old," Tammi reassured me. "You just need a little exercise to get you in shape to keep up."

"Yeah, well, I'm old enough to know you're going to be more trouble. Just a different kind, is all," I admitted.

"In that case, I'm hoping you'll enjoy being in trouble again."

"We'll see."

Tammi took the beanie hanging off her backpack, fastened it under her chin, and climbed on behind me. I punched the button, nicked down to first gear and eased on the throttle. Her thighs tightened against me, gripping hard. This wasn't her first rodeo on a motorcycle.

I did a quick check for headlights in the rearview. There was nothing but a bright orange glow reflecting. Without slowing down I took a wide turn onto the 86 and headed north.

I was on the run with a woman I barely knew. "You want to go by the casino and tell them you quit?"

"They'll figure it out eventually."

It worked for me. "Anywhere special you want to be?"

"There's a little place up on the 62 I danced at for a month or six weeks. It's in the middle of nowhere. We'd probably like it there for a while."

"Are you talking about the strip club that used to have the pretty good pizza place out in front?"

"Yeah, that's the place. Used to?"

"It's closed."

"In that case I know another off the 215 in Colton.

It's kind of nowhere if you like the burbs."

"Wait. We?" I was listening, too. She leaned back against the bagger's trunk, settled in and wrapped her legs around my waist.

"Yes, Frank. We. As in you and me. I don't see anybody else around. Do you?"

Trouble. Most times it's bad. Sometimes it's good. One way or another, it always seemed to find me, for better or worse. This time, I was thinking it was going to be for the better.

How could it not?

13

It was only a few hours ago when we were forced to listen to the sound of a hit-man's double tap. It boomed past the cheap tin walls of Jade's trailer in Bombay Shores. After witnessing the fire engulfing the trailer, I was smart enough to know I could be next. I went on the run with Tammi Dominga, Jade's neighbor, riding bitch on the back of my bagger. Both of us were on a mad dash to put miles on the clock.

I took us north, in a crazy rush and maybe too eager to put as many miles in the rearview as I could. Better safe than sorry was all I could think. Distance made for safety. Consent checking the review for headlights told me we were home-free.

We rolled into Banning. Emotionally exhausted from what we witnessed and physically drained from the constant back and forth yelling past the rushing air for most of the ride, we needed a break. We needed to talk about our next move. Would we go into the bright lights and big city of El Lay, or head for somewhere else?

There was no doubt it was easier to get lost in the

city. On the ride up, Tammi committed to taking up the dance circuit again. It would be a means to quick cash. I wouldn't be the one to say no. I was flat broke and easily convinced.

I pulled off the 10 into the familiar Farmer's lot and shut down. After the long ride, it would give the woman a chance to wash away the asphalt perfume. If Tammi was going to hit the dance-club circuit searching for work, a little food and a quick sprucing-up wouldn't hurt.

I waited for her to climb off the back seat. I purposely avoided mentioning anything about what we witnessed in Bombay Shores. "How long did you work at the place we're headed for?" I asked as I eased the heavy bagger onto its kickstand.

"The El Diablo? A couple of months. It started to get a little weird toward the end so I moved on."

"Weird? How?" I wanted to know.

"The usual. Drugs. It started slow at first. The club owner began dealing out the back door. Things got worse when he became mixed up with a cartel. No one figured on that. From there it all went bad. Fast."

She took a breath and went on without looking at me.

"The bouncers let in anyone who tipped them. The customers were getting worse. Unruly and touchy-feely. Thinking we'd all go home with them. The girls got tired of getting hit on constantly with no one to back us up. A lot left and never looked back.

High turnover for the dancers, and for good reason. Most of what she said sounded like strip-club par for the course, minus the drugs and cartel involvement. Still, working under those conditions had to be a major disadvantage to staying safe and getting paid.

"And you want to go back there to work? Do you think that's a good idea?"

"I want to have a look at the place. I've been wondering who's left from the old days."

The old days? She was gone for six months. How old could a day be? "If you're going to show up they'll want to see the old Tammi. You want me to get your bag so you can pretty up?

"That's all right. I'll get it. Don't leave without me."

Don't leave without her? Who the hell has she been hanging out with? I was starting to think there was more to this fast getaway of ours than met the eye.

The familiar click-clack of heels on hard tile floor perked up the ears of a couple of die-hard customers in the almost-empty diner. I caught myself looking around, wondering what the waitress with the sore feet looked like. Instead, my eyes ended up assaulted by Tammi, determinedly striding toward our table. She looked like she just stepped out of a spa makeover.

She tucked something that might have been a phone into a pocket on her backpack before slinging it over her shoulder. Long, bare legs looked good in high-heels. If her hips could move the way they did from the front, there was no telling what they were capable of doing in back.

I knew a woman could whip up miracles with a comb, a brush and a little makeup. This one transformed herself. No longer was she a disheveled, wind-blown woman riding bitch on the back of my ride. With a face all made up and lipstick-adorned lips, Tammi looked to be more than ready to take on the strip-club world.

In barely minutes, the woman transformed herself into a wide-eyed, dreamy-looking, long-legged dancer. Her legs ran all the way up to her short jean skirt and beyond. I couldn't believe my eyes—or my good fortune.

She regarded me with a warm smile and a come-hither look. My kind of woman.

"How soon can I start stuffing bills into your panties?"

She stuck her tongue out. "Honey, when I dance I don't wear panties."

That was good enough for me. I reached into a pocket, emptied it, and slapped the last of my cash on the table while Tammi made her way to the bike. I made sure to bring up the rear.

I wasn't disappointed.

The El Diablo didn't look so inviting. A street light shone down revealing the cracked brick exterior. It leaned at odd angles in a couple of places. Multiple coats of faded, peeling paint revealed cheap wood-panel walls separated by cheesy brick pillars.

The neon sign on the flat roof didn't look much better. It blinked rhythmically around unlit letters that appeared to be barely hanging on. Against the dark night sky it looked as though it would tumble off the roof at any minute.

From what I saw so far, the place looked to be in need of a major reno, and that was only the outside. If the inside held true to form, it would take a nice warm fire to fix all of its problems. It would be the best makeover the El Diablo could hope to get.

I turned off the street and took us into an alley toward the parking lot in back. I rode through without stopping. The only illumination came from an old overhead in a far corner. Cracked glass on the ground beneath the others meant they'd likely been shot out. In the dim light I could see the lot full of tricked-out motorcycles and half-tons. Plenty of cash parked out back.

I kept going and pulled to a stop in front of the building's double doors. Bouncers checked out the woman and the bike. They didn't bother with me.

"Do you know them?"

"None of them look familiar. Don't go far. I don't think I'm going to be long."

A bouncer approached and gave us stink-eye. Tammi climbed off, grabbed her backpack, and strode past him to the door. She leaned into the second man and said something I couldn't hear. He pulled open the door and she disappeared into an explosion of music and flashing lights. Minutes later she returned, and right away I knew she wouldn't be performing in this dump.

"The old manager is gone. This one looks even worse. He's drugged out and just plain ugly."

"Well then, where to next, baby? We've got a full tank." I fueled up in Banning before hitting the road.

"There's another place up in Fontana. One of the girls here told me the club was hiring."

"No problem. We're there."

Tammi climbed on and I punched the button and hit first gear. I snaked our way past cars parked in the street. The traffic lights didn't do me any favors until I finally hit the 10 and there were none. I picked up the pace. We'd be somewhere else soon enough.

I turned my head and Tammi bent hers to put an ear against my lips. "Did you notice the guy standing beside that gray pickup out back?"

She shook her head.

"I couldn't get a real good look in the dark, but I thought he looked like Buddy." I checked her reflection in the rearview. Nothing. No reaction at all but for her response.

"You're kidding, right? What would Buddy be doing there?"

I had no idea. "I wonder if he heard what happened to Jade."

"I don't want to know. Do you?" she asked.

"Not really. We cut it close to make it out of town with our lives. I don't want to stir the pot. I'm thinking Buddy would be a whole lick of trouble for both of us." Especially if he thought we made off with Jade's stash of cartel coca. I had enough of Buddy and I only met him once when I cold-cocked him in Jade's living room.

"The cops raided El Diablo about six months ago," Tammi said. "The owners were dealing drugs. Some of the girls were selling. Four of them got lucky and were able to get into rehab on account of it all."

"Were you close with any of them?" I wondered.

"No, I never ran with that crowd."

"That's a good thing. Did you hear how rehab went for the lucky ones?"

"I really don't know. I was never a part of it," she said.

Did I just ask a trick question? Her response came quick enough. Maybe she was telling the truth. If that was the case, why was I beginning to wonder?

My eyes kept wandering to the rearview and it wasn't out of riding habit. I worried Buddy might be on to us after spotting the definite look-alike in the El Diablo parking lot. In the dark I couldn't be certain he'd picked up our trail, but that didn't mean I couldn't keep an eye out.

If it was Buddy. It was dark in the lot, after all, and I could be wrong. I told myself I couldn't chance it. I changed speed. Split lanes in the wide bagger. Weaved in and out of traffic. Checked the rearview so many times I swear I was seeing things.

There was method to my madness. I was trying to draw out a silver half-ton looking like the one I spotted in the El Diablo lot. Sure, there would be a lot of them. This was L.A. Even so, I wanted to be cautious. If Buddy was out for revenge, I didn't want to give him the chance to get some.

It took some skillful riding, but it worked. I caught a silver truck closing on us. The driver, whoever he was, worked slow, almost unnoticeable at first. I kept my speed even, waiting him out. Was it Buddy? I'd know soon enough if I stayed patient.

I was working on the assumption that there was something going on. I just didn't know what. I only knew it started after the visit to the strip club. I didn't know anyone there. The woman hanging onto to me did. I didn't need a map for that. I turned my head to Tammi one more time. "Do you have any former El Diablo boyfriends that might have recognized you?"

There was still a chance it was a random truck. There had to be thousands on the road. She bent her head to me. Her lips moved against my ear. "There's always a guy who wants to make a connection. None of them ever stalked me that I know about."

No doubt that was true. How many times had I taken a liking to a dancer with a nice smile and a quivering ass, only to forget about her when I left the club, never to return?

"Is there any reason why Buddy might want to make that connection with you? Or with us?"

"I never knew Buddy all that well. He was into Jade, but she didn't bring him around when they were together. They pretty much kept to themselves."

I wondered how much of that was true. I remembered how Jade couldn't wait to introduce me to this one. I waited for her go on.

"They probably didn't want anyone around because of the drugs. I guess it's true what they say."

"What would that be?" I looked at her reflection in the mirror and waited.

"That it makes you paranoid." She shifted on the seat behind me.

"I guess. I wouldn't know." I checked the reflection in the mirror one more time. She bit her lip and turned away. Was she avoiding looking into my eyes?

"What are we going to do if it is Buddy, Frank?"

I had the answer for that. "Not a thing. We'll let him make the first move."

"I'm glad you're confident. I wouldn't know what to do."

I was confident, all right. Confident something was going on that didn't include me. What the hell did I know about this woman with her legs wrapped around me riding bitch on the back of my ride? Nada. Nothing. Well, that, and she looked outstanding in a t-shirt and a short skirt. For all I knew, Tammi could be packing another couple of keys in her backpack and I wouldn't be any the wiser.

Traffic on the 10 was busy and steady. It made it difficult to keep the truck in sight. It would appear and then disappear, falling behind cars and trucks. Whoever was doing the driving knew what he was doing.

"Take the Riverside exit north. It's coming up on your right," Tammi told me.

My passenger knew where she was going. That was a bonus I wasn't expecting from a small-town girl. I checked the mirror. The half-ton was gaining on us, fast.

"Baby, put your feet on the pegs and hang on tight. That truck I've been watching is about to go by on the left."

Tammi unhooked her ankles and lowered her feet to the footrests. Her arms tightened their grip. I twisted the wick to stay ahead while I made for the number four lane. I kept left in the lane and prepared to ride on. I checked the mirrors, and then turned to look over my shoulder. Nothing but empty freeway and a lonely silver half-ton. It was still gaining.

If the driver was psychic—

"When he goes by, try to get a look at the driver or any markings on the truck."

In the mirror Tammi's reflection turned to look. Her arms hugged me hard. Her thighs tightened on my hips. She called out. Her voice was high-pitched and panicky. "His window is down." She screamed. "He's coming toward us!"

At the last minute I steered across the lane onto the

exit ramp. My mirrors filled with an exploding blaze of orange light.

"Holy shit," Tammi exclaimed. "Did you see that?"

I didn't need to think about it. I already knew. "He threw a firebomb. It missed." I felt the need to tell her.

I made good on my escape from the freeway onto the exit too late for the truck driver to do anything about it. He roared past, forced to remain on the 10.

"What the hell was that about? Did you get a look at the driver?" I wanted to know.

Tammi's face was frozen in fear. She could only shake her head. There was nothing right about this deal. What had I missed in the last couple of days? If that was Buddy, he had to have a reason for tossing firebombs. Given his connection to Jade and the way he crashed into her living room, I'd say it was about missing drugs.

I knew I didn't have any.

14

L a Bonita's neon sign was like night and day compared to that of El Diablo. It fairly lit up the night for what seemed like a city block, at least. All the letters worked, too. I didn't need direction from Tammi to find the parking lot out back of the place. Plenty of light showed the way.

Even so, I wanted to know what I was going to be walking into. I did a circuit and rode through the parking lot like I knew where I was going. It was lit up like a mall parkade. Plenty of vehicles were high-end, but there was quite a collection of regular stuff, too. The mix seemed to me like it would be a good thing.

So far, La Bonita looked like nothing resembling a dump. The difference was quite noticeable and I wasn't even inside. Their huge, expensive-looking neon sign flashed up drinks and girls in a wild explosion of light and color. There was even valet parking out front. I stopped and a bouncer gave me the sign to shut down.

In my experience it wouldn't be the first time bikers weren't welcome at a strip club. A loud squeal of recognition for the mountain of a man approaching was all it took for hell to break loose. Tammi jumped off the back of my ride so fast I thought she was running away. In her haste she tripped, and the giant of a man caught her in his open arms. She flung her legs around him and screamed again as he carried her, dancing in circles, up the steps.

That left two of us standing around doing nothing. "I'm Frank. The good-looking one wrestling with your friend is Tammi Dominga."

A look of recognition crossed his face. "Dominga? I've heard that name mentioned around here. You can call me Bull."

Bull was no midget, either. He was almost as big as the one doing the dance routine with Tammi. I tipped my head toward her. "She's looking for work. What are the chances?"

He turned to watch the pair do their dance on the steps. "I heard somebody say Dominga was a pretty popular dancer back more than a few months. I never saw her perform. From what I heard I'd say the chance could be good."

"Judging by the reception out here, I think you might be right." I called out to the struggling couple making their way up the dance club's front steps. "Hey you two, are you going to bump crotches all night?"

The giant deposited Tammi at the top. She called out introductions. "This is Dawg. The guy beside you is Bull. They're the guys you need to know if you want your bike to stay put when you're not on it."

Bull stuck out his hand and I took it. He had a grip like a drill-rig roughneck. I let him see me wince. I was no pussy, but I figured the new guy might as well try to make some points. I got the okay to leave the bike where it was and I followed Tammi into the club.

When a woman walked into a strip club, men noticed. A woman that looked like Tammi was no exception. Plenty of eyes turned in her direction as her long legs and ass-shaking gait took her past tables. I couldn't fault her. She was only doing the job she knew.

Someone who looked important appeared to recognize her the minute she got half-way across La Bonita's carpeted floor. The manager. Already he was making his way. It had to be the earpieces on the bouncers outside calling in a warning, but even so. He was on her like a dog on a fire hydrant, and I don't mean he was doing any pissing.

I caught up to hear the man go to work. He began machine-gunning questions. Where have you been? Who's the guy on the motorcycle? Is he your boyfriend? Husband? Are you living together? Is this a social call, or are you looking for work? That last was all business from what I could hear in the noise of booming music and yelling, fist-pumping men doing what they were paying to do as they went on appreciating the on-stage flesh.

Before long, some of the other dancers recognized Tammi. They had to be regulars. I figured that was a good sign. She ended up surrounded by a mob. In minutes it turned into old home week. The crowd of scantily-clad women ignored the evil eyes coming from the paying customers. Their hard-earned cash didn't include down-time for the women who pushed away from their tables and halted lap-dances mid-thrust.

The girls didn't seem to mind. No one complained. It looked to me like Tammi was everybody's favorite and she hadn't even started to work yet.

She paraded across the floor and the applause followed. Quite a few in the crowd recognized her. Even the manager stood back and beamed. She must have been a money-maker. I wondered if he might have had a thing for her, because he appeared pretty pleased that his prodigal dancer had returned.

Tammi's stroll past the tables ended when the manager waved her over. She returned with a huge grin pasted across her face.

"How do you feel about getting up and doing a set?"

She shrugged, but she looked pleased. "Vince, I've been riding bitch and wearing asphalt perfume out on the freeway. The last time I washed my face was hours ago. Do you really want me to go on-stage looking like this?"

I thought I already knew the answer.

"Ladies, take her into the dressing room and get her set up," Vince instructed.

"That sounds like a yes. Who's the DJ?" she asked.

"It's still Ray."

I figured I might as well make myself useful. "I'll get your backpack."

Startled, as though suddenly reminded I was still around, Tammi turned and almost stumbled. "No, I'll get it." She rushed off to retrieve the backpack. She came back and disappeared into the back of the club followed by several of the other dancers. The manager, Vince, stayed behind and we stood around sizing each other up. He asked a lot of questions, maybe even too many.

"Where are you from? Do you have a job? How

long have you known Tammi?" he wanted to know.

He seemed to be a protective son of a bitch, but that was all right with me. If Tammi was a moneymaker for the club in the past, who was I to put a damper on things? I turned myself into Mr. Nice Guy and answered as best I could.

"How did you two meet?"

I left that one alone. The explanation would take too long. Besides, I figured Tammi could give him her own answer when she was ready. He must have thought I was all right, because it looked to me like he was beginning to relax.

"You ever do any bouncing?"

That one came out of nowhere. I'm not a small guy, but after seeing Dawg and Bull out front I knew bouncing wasn't ever going to be my strong point in a place as busy as this. I figured he already knew that. I wasn't about to bullshit the man.

"Not a bit. I'm not built for that. I'm more of a talker."

"Oh, you mean bullshitter. That's all right with me."

It was okay with me, too. If that was a test, I didn't mind taking it. He called my bluff.

"It's time La Bonita had a greeter at the front door and on the floor. I need someone to schmooze the crowd and give the money-spending customers that pay our salaries the recognition they deserve. Dawg and Bull do a good job for what they do, but they're a little rough around the edges. How are your edges?"

"I can fit in. What I don't know I'll learn fast." How hard could it be to bullshit with paying customers and help them pay more?

This all had to be because of Tammi, but hell, I didn't care. I needed a job too. Then Vince really put it to me.

"The club has an apartment on the ground floor. It's remodeled and soundproofed. One bedroom. Mostly furnished. There's access from a stairwell in the club and an outside door, but it's private. You interested?"

I considered for about the length of a New York minute. It would be like living next door to work, but I wasn't going to say no. How the hell could I refuse? I didn't even ask about the rent. "All right, I'll take it. But on one condition."

Vince looked about ready to change his mind. His eyes narrowed.

"What would that condition be?"

I knew by his tone the man wasn't accustomed to listening to conditions. He had to be wondering who the hell would put one on a furnished one-bedroom in El Lay.

"Don't tell Tammi. I want to surprise her. I need some time to pick up a few things. You're going to have to keep her working for a while tonight." I knew by the sly smile Vince wouldn't say no. We shook hands and the deal was done.

"Wait here while I get the key, Frank. If you take the job you can start work tomorrow on the late afternoon shift. Show up early and I'll fill you in on what I need from you."

I took the key. I took the job, too.

15

I unlocked the door to the apartment and walked into a brand-new life. I had a new woman. I had a new job. I had a place for us to stay while we made a bit of money. What could go wrong with that? I gave myself an attaboy and mimed patting myself on the back for good measure.

I was only a few days out of Mexico and already it felt like a month with everything that happened. El Lay was as good a place as any to hole up. I had a roof over my head, even if it was a strip-club roof.

What were the chances anyone would come looking for two people who had nothing to do with Jade's drugs?

Eager to get the place ready, I rode off to pick up sheets and towels and a shower curtain. I found some ribbon for a bow to hang on the door. I made the bed, dropped the towels in the bathroom and hung the curtain.

The grocery store came next. I stocked the fridge and washed the dishes and neated the place up. If I was going to be doing the mattress dance with Tammi, I figured on serenading her a bit by making it look like I could contribute.

I had to admit, the reaction I witnessed when Tammi walked into the club took me by surprise. I knew she was a good-looking beauty with her long, shapely legs and slim, busty frame. The long dark hair worked to her advantage, too. What I didn't have an appreciation for were her abilities on the dance floor and working the pole.

Many of the customers seemed to know her—at least as well as they could know a performer. They were happy she was about to be dancing again. It was like she had never left. Obviously she had been a popular dancer. That meant she had been a money-maker for the club. There'd be no holding her back.

Even so, after our long day, food and sleep would probably be high on the list when she dragged her tired ass home. I went to work on a pot of spaghetti sauce. I slapped together some meatballs and threw them into the frying pan. If all that didn't earn me points, there'd be no telling what would.

Satisfied with my labors, I cleaned up before strolling nonchalantly into the club. I planted myself at an empty table in a dim corner a long way from the stage. I kept my back to the wall where I liked it. I leaned back to watch the action in the club. In no time a beer appeared.

"That's from Vince," the server told me.

I barely noticed her when I turned to look behind the bar to wave my thanks. The woman turned to walk away.

"Wait a minute." I reached into a pocket as she

turned. I took a better look when she leaned over to be heard in the noisy club.

"There's no need to be reaching for anything. It's on the house."

My eyes roamed. It was an old habit. There was no telling what was underneath the loose clothes. She was cute, though. And there were possibilities lurking, I was sure of that. Better than that, she might be someone I could talk to about the club and its reputation.

"I was reaching for a tip. Is that allowed?" I smiled.

The look of surprise said I must have made a good first impression. You never know when you might need something. If all it took was a tip, I figured I was starting out in a pretty good place with this one.

She picked up the money and walked away, but not in an obvious way. She had a long, comfortable stride. Her hips didn't sway. The black pants covered up nice long legs by the look of it. I liked long legs. Hell, truth be known, I liked them short, too. Or any way I could get them.

The corner table gave me a good view of the huge floor and I went back to looking over the club. Three stages glowed under the lights. I couldn't count all the tables. I'd have to stand on a chair to do that.

The stand-up bar stretched a long way against a wall. It made sense that there were no seats. There was no use when you want the customers sitting at tables to buy their lap dances. Private rooms looked to be off to the rear of the club.

The server showed up to interrupt my thoughts with another beer. "Girl, I'm a watcher, not a drinker" I told her.

"It's on the house again. No tip necessary."

"If you say so. But there is one thing I'd like to know."

"You're not going to ask me out, are you? We're not allowed to date the customers."

I looked her straight in the eye. "What's your name?"

"Danielle."

"Well now, Danielle, if I wasn't already attached to the most beautiful and talented woman in the place," I told her, "you'd be my choice for that long blonde hair you have all tied up and out of sight. Those bright green eyes are downright pretty, too. Not only all that, but you're a real treat to watch when you walk away."

Even in the dim light of the bar it was evident she was turning pink. I looked her up and down. I always did the first time. Too bad about that loose top. The way she wore it, it might be hiding plenty. Or not. By the time I finished, the poor girl was beet-red, but she hadn't left yet, either.

Yeah, I was being a bit of a pig. Call me out on it, but anyone in a strip club would be, including me. Besides, the girls were accustomed to it. They were waiting tables in a strip club with naked women dancing on multiple stages.

"Mister, I don't know who you are or who you're here with, but you sure talk a good line. I know, because I've heard my share in this place."

"In that case, I'll stop when I'm ahead."

She smiled. I smiled back. Another Mexican standoff. They seemed to be coming along on a regular basis. I figured working in a place like this she heard so many bad lines that one more wouldn't gain me a thing.

"If you get a minute, would you tell Dominga that

there's a man over here who'd like to see her?"

"Just so you know, the dancers aren't allowed to date customers either."

"Thanks again. I'll remember that."

I took some side eye as Danielle walked away and disappeared. She reappeared out of a side door off the stage with Tammi in tow. I wasn't so far away and the light wasn't so bad that I couldn't see the expression on Tammi's face. It's funny how a frown about erases everything else.

Danielle pointed in my direction and Tammi paraded across the floor. The whistling and clapping began all over. The see-through gown tried to cover the assets, but it didn't hide much. She appeared naked beneath but for the flesh-covered bra and g-string. For sure the tips would be good tonight.

Every step Tammi took had the room in a frenzy as she sashayed past crowded tables. She stopped at a couple when she recognized past customers, just as they remembered her.

She was definitely all woman, and a good-looking one too—maybe too good-looking for her own good. She had everything in all the right places. Her practiced movements emphasized it with every step.

The woman was obviously in her element as a performer. Now I knew why she was one of Vince's favorites. She had it all going on and she knew how to flaunt it. The crowd loved her for it.

"It took you long enough to get here. I thought you were going to stop and pick up some cash on the way." I wondered if she thought I could be jealous.

"I have to let people know I'm back, Frank. A stroll through the crowd is as good a way as any to do that."

She hugged me and sat down.

"How does it feel to be back in the business?"

"I don't know if I missed it or not," Tammi said.

"Judging by the reactions you're getting from the customers. I'd say they missed you."

"Have you seen me dance?" She perked up.

"Not yet. I just got here a few minutes ago."

She looked puzzled. "Where were you?"

"I'm not talking. It's a surprise."

She changed tack mid-conversation. What woman couldn't? "I see you met Danielle. She told me you were trying to sweet-talk her. Were you?"

"She made a point of telling me she wasn't allowed to date customers."

"You didn't answer me. Did you ask her out?"

"I sent her to get you, didn't I? I have a surprise for you. Do you want it now, or later." Okay, so it was sounding like I needed to pop the surprise right now.

"How about now. I don't like to wait." Raised eyebrows and an impatient, hard look convinced me.

"I talked to Vince. He was trying to figure us out, and what the hell you're doing with me. When he was done he must have been happy with what he heard."

"Why?"

"He offered me a job."

"Did you take it?" she wanted to know.

"Of course."

Impatience turned to joy. Tammi squealed and jumped on my lap. It seemed like everyone in the place was looking our way. That included Danielle. I hoped she was just a little disappointed. I didn't care about the droolers.

Behind the bar Vince wagged a finger. So much for

the no touching the dancers rule, but he was grinning.

"About that motel we were planning on staying at tonight."

"Is it full?"

Tammi didn't look so happy now. It was a long day for both of us. Witnessing what happened to her friend Jade couldn't have been much fun either. We were exhausted from the night's long ride to make good our escape. "No. I didn't make a reservation."

"Frank, we need somewhere to stay until we find a place." She was definitely annoyed. Narrowed eyes and crossed arms said so.

"I know. I already found us a place."

"You did? Where?" She didn't believe me, but I didn't care.

"Right here. Ground floor. You can check it out when you get off. If it's not good enough it will give us time to look for something else."

Tammi squealed again and jumped on me one more time for good measure. Bull started making his way over. I figured he had to show the customers that touching the dancers was a no-no, even if it was only me. House rules were house rules.

Bull arrived at the table and Tammi didn't waste a second. She climbed off me and settled on him like he was her long-lost brother. Or something. He blushed and grinned like a teenager on his first time in a strip club. Or maybe a candy store with naked women in it.

Behind the bar, Vince picked up the microphone. "Gentlemen and ladies, management would like to announce La Bonita's newest dancer for your pleasure. Give Dominga a round of applause."

DJ Ray held up a hand. When he brought it down,

Tammi's play list began blaring over the speakers. Bull set Tammi down and she began twirling her way through the crowded floor past the packed tables. She climbed the steps to center stage. On each one, she halted and turned to face the crowd. The screaming, fist-pumping crowd definitely approved.

It was time for me to get to see what everyone else seemed to already know. I stood up as Danielle threaded her way through the tables in my direction. She was just in time as Tammi reached the top of the stage. I sat back down and waited.

"I hear that one is a real sweetheart. Do you want another beer?"

Tammi waved over the crowd. I was unsure if she was waving at me or the packed tables.

"No thanks. It's time for me to be getting out of here." I moved to reach into my pocket.

"I already told you, no tipping." Now I had two women annoyed with my antics.

Tammi glared in my direction. It wasn't me getting the stink-eye this time. I smiled up at Danielle. This time she didn't smile back.

"Tammi sent me over to tell you she'll be bringing some of the girls over to meet you when the club closes."

"Will you be coming?" I wanted to know.

"No. I can't."

"I'd like it if you did," I let her know.

She shook her head and mouthed a definite *No*.

It was just as well. The last thing I needed was another woman in my life. One-on-one had always been the safest bet for me.

I didn't have to remember my lies if I never told any.

16

When I heard Tammi's invitation, I had no idea what deal would end up at our apartment. I left the club to make sure the place would be ready. I stacked plates and laid out cutlery for a full house. Satisfied my preparations would make a good impression, I stretched out on the sofa to wait it out.

My eyes closed, but I couldn't sleep. I kept considering the possible sighting of Buddy in El Diablo's dark parking lot. I rehashed it, over and over. Tammi had to be right when she said the place was a hangout for druggies. Was Buddy selling, or buying?

Given what happened back in Bombay Shores I shouldn't have been surprised to see Buddy in the lot. But was it really Buddy? I had no reason to think it could be.

A sixth sense, maybe. Surely not more than that.

The firebomb tossed our way on the 10 definitely had my attention. At worst, it was an attempt at murder. At the least, it was a warning, and an obvious one. But there was a problem with both assumptions. I had no enemies that I knew about, especially in this part of the world. Who was it directed toward? I didn't want to think about it, but I couldn't let it go.

Tammi was the only other person. She was the obvious unknown in the equation. I needed to take a ride out to El Diablo—the sooner the better. I had to do it for my own peace of mind, even if I didn't learn anything new.

There was a problem with doing that. I had a job and somewhere I had to be. Unfortunately, the job Vince offered was going to have to wait. Trying to find out who was throwing gasoline bombs was more important.

At least, it was to me.

I wrestled with whether or not to tell Tammi. She was in good with Vince. Whether he'd cut me some slack because of her was another matter. I'd make a try at explaining what happened last night in person—that is, if Vince didn't fire my ass before I got started.

Finally, my brain stopped working and I dozed off.

Loud voices accompanied by peals of laughter and scantily-clad women crowding through the door announced the arrival of our guests. It was definitely a crowd. They were all here.

There was nothing shy about them, either. Most came fresh off the dance floor and in costume. Halter tops, g-strings, short-shorts and high-heels slithered through the door in single file. They were all packing bags like it was a sleepover. What man wouldn't pay a premium for eye candy like that?

The questions came fast and loose.

"Where is he?"

"Look at all that food. Is he taken? I need a cook."

"You better not let this one get away."

"Are you two just dating, or are you living-together partners?"

"When you get tired of him, can I have him?"

Tammi rolled her eyes in my direction in time to see me puff out my chest. She burst out laughing and I got the reaction I wanted. We both knew I wouldn't be going anywhere with any of them.

Chairs shuffled. Women sat down. Conversation halted. Oohs and ahhs took over. Plates were loaded. Bread was passed around. Then came silence. I had never seen it happen before. The women stopped talking and started chewing all at once. I struggled to keep the plates filled. Bread turned out to be in short supply.

"Well, now I know how to satisfy the lot of you and keep you happy at the same time. That's got to be a first for any man."

"You better learn their names if you're going to let them take you home. And you can just put your eyes back in your head."

I didn't skip a beat. "Don't be a spoil-sport. I only have eyes for you."

"Yeah, and I was born yesterday."

Hell, Tammi was by far the best-looking woman in the place. She had no worries there. I stood up to address the crowd. "Ladies, I have to admit I've never seen so many good-looking woman-parts all together in one tiny space."

Laughter erupted. High fives made their way around the table.

"Now here comes the house rules." Confused looks spread across the faces of the women, including

Tammi's. "I think by now you know you're welcome here, any time, day or night. However, I'm a man, and as past experience and we all know, even a man with good intentions can be sorely tempted."

"Yeah baby, we know it, too. Earth men are easy," someone called out. More high-fives made their way around the table accompanied by laughter.

"Like I said, any time, day or night. There's a bedroom down the hall. If you don't change in the club before you come over, you're going to have to change in there. Keep it neat and stay dressed when you're here."

The women turned to Tammi. There were more shocked looks than I could count. "Where the hell did you find this guy? He's too good to be true and we all know it."

Tammi's arm snaked around me. "He's all mine. Don't any of you forget it."

"All right, ladies. Who wants more garlic bread?" Somehow, I came up with another loaf that must have slipped away earlier. They ignored me. I didn't mind. I was grinning like I shouldn't.

"Garlic bread? Man, get us some rope, a tarp and a car with an empty trunk. We need somewhere to put Tammi while the rest of us take turns bringing you home."

The party was over. The apartment was empty. We were alone and even more exhausted. I turned out the light.

"No. Leave it on," Tammi said. "Come over here. I want you to see something, and then I want to see something." Tammi reached back to unhook her top and tossed it on the floor. Okay, so maybe I wasn't so tired after all. Her breasts sure as hell didn't move an inch. A forearm strategically placed covered just enough. I almost ruptured my eyes trying to get a better look. Then she dropped her arm and let me have both barrels in a full frontal.

"You like?" she wanted to know. She arched her back. Nothing moved.

"Oh yeah. And you know it."

"I can tell. Now get over here. I've waited long enough to get a look at what that woman couldn't stop talking about."

I knew which woman she meant. She unzipped me and dipped her hand in to check. She undid my belt and yanked my pants down. I stepped out of them and turned to face her.

"Ohh. Look at that—and it's only half-way there," she said. She circled me with her hand and looked up. Her mouth opened wide and she was on me, fast, all at once. It felt like she was trying to swallow me whole. It took her more than a while to come up for air. I didn't complain. "I need to breathe," she apologized.

"As long as you're happy."

"I'm happy right now with what I have in my hand. I'm pretty sure I'll be even happier in a few minutes." She hung on and pulled me toward the bedroom.

The willing woman in bed with me wasn't the only thing on my mind. I had some fast talking to do, now or never, and I knew it was bound to interrupt the proceedings. "I have something I need to do tomorrow. You're going to have to play nice with Vince. If I'm lucky he'll still have a job for me when I get back."

She withdrew her head. "When you get back? From

where? What's up?" She looked down and giggled. "Besides this."

"I'm going to ride over to the Diablo to check it out."

Tammi didn't look happy to hear that. "What? Why? Why would you do that? You saw what it was like last night. It's a dump. It always has been."

If it was always a dump, why was she dancing there? "I need to know if that was Buddy hanging out in the parking lot." She still didn't look happy. She pushed off and sat up.

"But why? Are you planning on making him your new best friend?"

"I want to know if it was Buddy that threw the firebomb."

"Just because he might be there doesn't mean he was the one."

She was trying to convince me otherwise. If that was true, then who was it? I still needed to know about Buddy. "If it wasn't Buddy, I want to at least try to find out who it was and why he was trying to set you on fire."

I was already convinced. Tammi wasn't. Her eyes grew bigger. She threw the sheet off and jumped out of bed. "Me? You were on the bike too."

She began pacing back and forth at the foot of the bed. She halted all of a sudden. A thoughtful look consumed her face.

"Yes, I was on the bike too. I've thought and re-thought the whole episode. I don't know anyone that would want to set me on fire—outside of Buddy, that is."

She crossed her arms over her breasts.

"He must have taken it personal when I whacked him upside the head after he scared the shit out of me when he broke into Jade's."

"Don't think so much. I don't want you at El Diablo, Frank. You saw it last night. It's dangerous."

"I saw the parking lot. I want to have a look inside. Maybe Buddy has a new place to hang out."

"That's enough talking about Buddy in this bed." Tammi climbed in and stretched the length of her long, firm body as she pressed against mine. A hand reached for me. "I haven't had enough of this. Can I have more?"

"You can have as much as you want." Changing the subject wasn't going to change my mind, no matter how hard Tammi tried.

She tried very hard.

17

I knocked on Vince's open office door. Respect worked for me, especially when I had to ask if I could show up late on my first official day of work. He looked up and smiled and waved me in. I figured it was fifty-fifty on whether he'd fire my ass.

"You must be anxious to get started. I like that."

"Yes, I am anxious to get started. Before I do, I have something I need to tell you. When I'm finished I'm going to ask for a favor." Vince's mouth turned down in a frown. Screw it. What I needed to do was important. At least, in my life it was important.

"Start talking." The man didn't waste time. He looked up from his paperwork and then went back to his calculator and his receipts.

"I know you like Tammi. The reception she got from you and the dancers made that obvious. Hell, even the bouncers are crazy about her. The customers even more. That's why I have to tell you what happened on the ride over here last night."

Vince looked up from the pile of receipts. His eyes

bored into mine. He pushed back from his desk and waited. I had his attention. I didn't want to give him a chance to ask questions.

"Someone in a silver half-ton threw a Molotov cocktail at us. He missed, obviously. I need to find out who it was and why he did it."

"You're not going to bring trouble here, are you, Frank? I don't want any trouble."

I didn't want to ruin what had turned into a good thing, either. I came in wondering how much I should tell Vince. Now I knew. He'd get the basics. "To be honest, I don't know anyone who hates me enough to want to set me on fire. Tammi, just might, but I don't know that for sure. I need to find out who's crazy enough to be throwing fireballs around."

"I can't have my best moneymaker in trouble," Vince said. "Find out what's up. I already told the staff about you. I'll make excuses if you don't get back in time to start your shift. You'll be on the clock, but I'm going to want to get paid back."

I offered my hand. "Thank you. We've got a deal."

I walked out of Vince's office on a high note. I gave my word. He took it at face value. He expected results. I would get him some.

During our talk between the sheets, Tammi made it plain she didn't want me visiting El Diablo. After last night's performance—both on-stage and off—it was better to leave her in bed and asleep. The woman knew exactly how to cajole me into getting her way.

I pulled a Bombay Shores and pushed my bagger into the street before hitting start. The noisy exhaust roared to life. I wasn't worried. I was far enough away that the rumbling pipes wouldn't wake her. I nicked into first and went looking for adventure I didn't want to find.

It was early, and I enjoyed the ride, even though I was in and out of traffic and half-asleep drivers trapped in their cages. It gave me time to think.

I didn't hold out a lot of hope after what I witnessed in El Diablo's parking lot the previous night. Even if the bikers knew the man, no one would be willing to tell a stranger anything about Buddy. Riding in on a motorcycle wasn't any guarantee. I was pretty sure they'd see me as just another independent, loyal to no one.

I approached El Diablo in the fresh light of day. It turned out to be an even bigger dump. A bonfire would be the best this place could hope for if anyone ever decided renovations were in order. Given the crowd, I don't think present management would look to rebuild—insurance payout or not.

It was eleven in the morning, and already ear-shattering music spilled out of the open back door. The parking lot was half-filled with motorcycles. They weren't here this early for a breakfast burrito. Smoke was in the air—probably in the veins too, but then that wouldn't be smoke. This place was heaven if you were looking to buy. Why it hadn't been shut down was anyone's guess.

Street-side, the place looked deserted. No surprise there, given what was going on out back. I backed to the curb and let my wheel rest against it. I wondered how long it was since someone walked in through the front door. I pushed it open and I had my answer. The music almost skipped a beat. My eyes located the raggedy-ass, wide-eyed DJ. His eyes fixated on me, and it looked as though he was ready to announce an incoming.

Maybe it was my imagination. I was more than a little jumpy.

Everything went back to normal—whatever normal was in a place that reeked of stale air, stale beer, and drugs. It wasn't my imagination. The place was definitely a dump. What was left of worn-out, dirty carpet covered an uneven floor. Beer was splattered over walls and stage. Here and there it looked to be mixed with blood. Damn, but did they never hose the place down?

The glass on the stage's filthy shower stall was so cloudy I could barely see through it. I doubted there would be a dancer fool enough to perform in that thing. If she kept her clothes on no one would know the difference.

A waitress on her way to a table circled around with an expectant look. I ordered a beer—hold the glass. The waitress didn't blink. She picked one off the tray and slammed it on the table in front of me. "Cash only. No tab."

"I can live with that." I let her see her tip. She made to reach for it but wasn't quick enough when I held on to it. I took a chance. "I'm looking for someone. An old friend. Name's Buddy. He drives a silver half-ton, maybe with a dent in the passenger door. You see him around lately?"

Biker women were notoriously silent to outsiders about their men—the ones they belonged to, and the ones they knew. I slipped the five on the table and told her she owned it. She picked it up and almost ran toward the bartender. So much for trying to be friendly.

Her lips barely moved as she mumbled something I couldn't hear. He looked my way to size me up and I must have passed the test. I took my beer with me. In this place it wouldn't last long sitting all by itself on an empty table.

"You the one looking for a guy?"

"That's me."

"Then you'd know his name."

Shit. Buddy's name. Had I actually been stupid enough to say I was looking for Buddy? Now I knew for sure I was on edge. "Yeah," I mumbled. My brain went into overdrive. What did Jade tell me when I had him down on the floor? "Grant. His name is Grant."

If he was smart enough to ask for a last name I'd be out of here so fast my head wouldn't have time to spin. When he didn't I figured he probably didn't know it either.

"He was here last night. He high-tailed it out the door so fast he didn't remember to pay his bill."

"You know where he lives?"

"Not a chance. He comes and goes. Where he goes I don't care."

I slapped a twenty on the bar. "Maybe this will take care of it." Yeah, and that twenty would end up in the bartender's back pocket so fast a magician couldn't spot the move.

"Who's looking?"

"Tell him it's Jade's friend from Bombay Shores."

If the bartender passed on the message it would get Buddy's attention. He'd know I was on to him—if he was the one who served up last night's fiery cocktail. If he wasn't, I was out of luck. The bartender's eyes digested the twenty. He could picture it in his pocket already.

"When do the dancers come on?" I asked for no reason in particular.

He bobbed his head toward the stage. They were trying for the lunch crowd. I looked around. From what I could see, the lunch crowd was somewhere else. "One is due right about now."

He swept the twenty off the bar.

I took a chance. "Does Tammi still dance here?"

"Tammi?"

"Yeah. You might know her by Dominga."

"Dominga. Yeah, I knew one by that name. A while ago now. She was trouble. Big trouble."

I laid another twenty on the bar. His hand made for it like a rabbit on a tear toward a vegetable patch.

"How so?"

The twenty disappeared as fast as the last one. "She got mixed up with a bunch of hard-cores out of Sinaloa on the Mexican side. She ended up almost getting a bunch of people killed for her trouble."

18

When I left La Bonita, I was hoping for the best about Tammi. After my visit with El Diablo's bartender, I knew the worst. I didn't want to believe she told a pack of lies concerning her past. Hell, I had my own lies to tell if I wanted to. Still, I knew now why she didn't want me checking up on her. She knew questions I had about Buddy would lead to questions about her, and that I wouldn't be liking the answers.

There was no going back. I needed to keep digging for my own piece of mind, but I needed time to digest what I learned at El Diablo. The time to do it was on the ride back to La Bonita, before I became distracted by Tammi and the business of the club.

At a light I spied an old-style diner. It would be just what I needed—a place to pause and reflect over apple pie and ice cream. If the pie was good I might make it a regular stop for more of the same.

I burned a U-turn and backed it up out front. I climbed off and stretched and climbed the steps. I pushed the door open. A tin bell hanging over the frame clanged to announce another customer.

A stool at the far end of the counter with a view out the window called my name. Positioned just right, I could keep an eye on my ride. If someone from the club told Buddy about my questions, I'd be able to watch my back. I wasn't eager to be on the receiving end of another gasoline bomb, even if it missed.

My thoughts were in overdrive from what I learned at El Diablo. Barely overnight, Tammi stopped being the innocent bystander. Now, it seemed like she might be a willing participant in Jade's demise. I was left to wonder how Buddy fit into the picture.

I was fairly confident I had the first part. Jade and Tammi crossed paths with someone and cheated them out of cartel coke—except when the cheating was done they probably didn't know who it belonged to. Had they been smart, the scorpion on the package would have clued them in.

But then, who was their victim?

Buddy broke into Jade's place expecting it to be empty. Instead, I was there to scuttle his attempt to retrieve the missing goods. Whoever it was ordered him to track down the drugs couldn't have been happy when he learned Buddy's search and retrieval didn't go so well.

Buddy probably dealt his last hand and spilled his guts about Jade holding the drugs. When the sicarios showed up to remedy Buddy's lapse, he would have ended up off the hook for the missing coca the sicarios found in Jade's closet.

Or maybe Tammi gave up the information to save her own ass. Depending on how well she could lie, cheat and steal, selling out Jade and implicating Buddy would keep her in the clear—for a while, at least.

That's where I came in as Tammi's flavor of the day. She saw an opportunity to get out of a ghost town and disappear. The fact that I was a stranger would make it harder for anyone to track her down. There was one problem with that. She went straight back to her old stomping ground using her real name.

How smart was that?

Unless she could pull someone else into her scam to take the heat off, she'd soon be dead meat, too. I was beginning to wonder if it was my turn in the hot seat.

There was one more thing I needed to figure out. I needed to know if Tammi was packing any drugs. So much for that fresh start I thought I deserved. Deep as I was into the well of misery I created for myself, I didn't hear the woman come up behind me. I was thinking too hard and feeling too sorry for myself.

"That's a nice ride you have out there. Mind if I take a look?"

I didn't bother to turn around. "Sure. Go ahead."

The cowbell clanged, and then it clanged again a couple of minutes later. Maybe now I'd get some service.

"I hope you don't mind. I threw a leg over to see what it felt like. It's too big for little old me."

I was in a hateful mood. I had no patience for some wannabe biker chick slinging hash in a diner. "I hope you're not wearing a short skirt. I don't want to have to wipe it down before I climb on."

I knew I shouldn't have said it the minute my mouth closed. My chin almost smacked against my chest as the follow-through from the backhander did its job. The woman hit the back of my head so hard it almost knocked me off the stool. I tried rubbing my head but it didn't do any good. She had to have plenty of practice with a move like that.

"That's no way to talk to a lady. Didn't anyone ever teach you manners? Or have you been on the road so long that manners you never had are gone with the wind?"

My head rang like a church bell on Sunday morning. With the waterworks streaming out of both eyes I could barely see. By the time I got it together and took a better look, the woman's hands were firmly on her hips and her feet were spread like a boxer's. It looked like she was trying to make up her mind whether I deserved another one for good measure.

I held up my hands in mock surrender and swiveled on the barstool to face my attacker. Her thigh blocked mine and kept me facing the counter. I had to resort to the mirror for a better look. Long blonde hung past her shoulders. Bright green eyes met mine in the mirror. I knew that woman.

"Danielle. Holy shit, woman. You pack a wallop. I'm sorry."

"Sorry doesn't cut it, jackass. This isn't a tacky strip joint and I'm not some piece of trash you just met. If you're expecting to get some service after that degrading little comment, you better shape up. If not, get out. The faster the better."

She waved a thumb over her shoulder toward the door. The cook stuck his head out the pass-through window. He glared in my direction. He didn't look pleased. He definitely wasn't happy to have his only waitress annoyed by a customer. "Is everything all right out there, Dani?"

"It's all good so far. I think I've got him cowed and backpedaling toward the door."

"In that case, after you chase the son of a bitch out, lock it behind him so he can't use the excuse of wanting to pay his bill to get back in."

Danielle turned off her smile and went back to glaring at me. "Well? I'm still waiting."

"You're not going to cut me any slack, are you?"

"Not one bit. You heard the man." Her eyes moved to the cook. "What's it going to be?"

The cook changed position and was leaning against the doorway to the kitchen. He held a huge knife clutched in one hand. It pointed at the ceiling. Arms were crossed over his barrel of a chest, but the knife was ready to go clutched in his outside hand.

"If you want me to leave and never come back, I can do that. Just say so. But you should know that I just got hold of some information that turned my world upside down. I'm not making excuses, and if I was I wouldn't expect sympathy anyway. I'm master of my own demise."

Christ, now I was using feeling sorry for myself to excuse my bad manners.

"That's a good start, but you're not done yet."

"When will I be done?" I wanted to know.

"I'll let you know."

No quitter, this one. I shifted my eyes, looking for the cook. He disappeared into the kitchen, taking his knife with him. I figured he was only out of sight enough to be listening.

"I've got a lot of thinking to do between now and when I get back to La Bonita. I was doing some of it while I was staring at the wall behind the counter. I wasn't paying attention to anything but my own stupidity. You handed me my ass on a platter. I'm not used to that." Would it work?

"I can tell. Even so, you need to know it takes a lot more than talk to make this woman forgive. Just so you know, I never forget."

I needed to start kissing some serious ass or I'd be flung out the door in about five seconds. "Can we have a do-over?" If that was the best I could come up with, I figured the door just got about half-way closer and all the way open. If I chanced it I could probably make it to the bike before she started flinging dishes at me.

"Is that what you want?"

I figured I better not think about it for too long. "Yes."

"Good. I'm Danielle. We crossed paths in the bar, remember? You might have forgotten my name when all those women ended up in your apartment last night."

She wouldn't be about letting up. At least she stuck out her hand and smiled. I shook it and smiled back. "Are we even?"

"Not yet, but now I'll let you start to work on getting there."

I'd come too close with this one. She wasn't about cutting me any slack. "I'll have some of that apple pie I spied by the register. A root beer float to go along with it would really take the edge off."

"You're not used to begging, are you?"

I couldn't help it. I gave her a full-face grin. No, and I'm not going to start now, even for you."

"Good to know."

Danielle retreated long enough to slide a plate with

a slice of pie covered in ice cream down the counter. It came to a halt in front of me. If I didn't know better, I'd say she was trying to kiss up, and that's what I told her. Now it was her turn to grin.

"I can't hold a grudge. And you look like you need some space. You'll get it for the time it takes to finish that pie."

I devoured it as fast as I could. I wanted to get the hell out before the woman crawled up behind me and stuck a knife in my back. At the register I put a hand in a pocket to dig out some cash.

"There you go, putting your hand in your pocket again. Don't bother. It's on me. So is the sore head. Just don't make it a habit."

"Well thanks. I'll remember that." How could I forget? I'd have another lump to remind me.

"You better. When I need payback, I'll let you know. You look like you're not in a hurry to be anywhere and I've got a break coming up. Let's take a walk."

She turned to the cook in back. "Eddy, I'm going on my break. Look after the place for me, all right?"

It became plain Eddy had been listening all along. "Yeah. No. Spinning that one a tale of woe doesn't look like it's going to get you a bigger tip."

"A bigger tip? It wouldn't take much to beat nothing," she grinned at Eddy.

"All right, you two. Enough with the picking on me."

"Come on, Frank. It's a nice day. I don't want to waste my break in here."

"You remembered my name." I was impressed.

"Your dancer friend told me all about you. How do

you like them apples? One more thing. I don't want anyone at the club knowing I wait tables here. This place is my secret. I guess it's ours now—if you don't burn me, that is."

"You can trust me. You want to go for a short ride?"

"No thanks. I don't ride bitch."

I was suitably chastised. "Well then. Let's walk and talk."

Danielle led us into an alley between tidy, fenced back yards and old, wooden garages. "I like working in that little diner. I get along with Eddy. He treats me like a daughter. I like that, too. The tips aren't great but the customers are."

"They always are in a neighborhood like this."

"I live not far from here. It's an easy walk back and forth."

"It's good to have a place to call home. I've been on the road for so long I pretty much forgot what it's like."

"I've got a boyfriend, Frank."

That came from out of nowhere. Maybe she could read me like a book after all. "I already have more on my plate than I can handle right now. Just because I know where you hide out doesn't mean I'll be back."

"That's up to you," she said. "Break time is over. You want me to wipe down your seat?"

Damn. This woman was something else. "The reason I've been walking behind you is so I can look without you knowing about it."

"Too late. I know."

"Then you already know you have great legs."

She turned to look at me. Her face glowed red. "I work the early shift. If you want conversation, come back whenever you want. If you're looking for anything more than that, I know you already have it waiting for you at the club and at home."

I stopped at the bottom of the steps. "Do you mind if I watch you from down here?"

Danielle reached the top and grinned. "You just did. I'd have been disappointed if your back was to me when I turned to look."

Danielle didn't seem to mind some mild flirting, either.

19

The respite I found at Eddy's diner thanks to bumping into Danielle was short-lived once I threw a leg over my bagger and hit the road. I needed to make up time if I wanted to keep Vince happy and start my new job at La Bonita. I lane-split when I had to and weaved in and out of heavy traffic. The bagger's wide bars tested my lane-splitting abilities more than a few times, and in the heavy traffic I knew why any biker worth his salt rode with narrow bars.

My mind wasn't on riding. It was on what I leaned from the Diablo's bartender. Tammi lied to me, and we were going to have a confrontation I couldn't put off. I arrived only to discover the apartment empty. It was probably for the better. Not wanting to face Tammi yet, I was somewhat relieved.

I cleaned up with a fresh shirt and jeans. I stopped by Vince's office to let him know I was back.

"Did you find out what you needed to know?" he asked, as soon as I stuck my head in the door.

"I think so. But I didn't come by to bother you

with that yet. I wanted to touch base so you could clue me in on what my job entails. It has to be more than schmoozing customers."

Vince settled back in his chair. "We have a few different crowds here—lunchtime, afternooners and night-time. That's all during the week," he explained. "Weekends are another matter."

I let him go on.

"The noon crowd—nooners, I like to call them—come in to eat and gawk, usually starting around 11:30. That crowd lasts until 1:30 or 2:00 at the latest, depending on when they get their lunch hour. Most have to get back to work eventually. There's nothing we can do about that."

I wasn't unfamiliar with the basics of a strip club. I spent plenty of time wasting hours and money in quite a few of them. I wasn't there to learn how they operated day-to-day, nor did I care.

"I know that was always the case with me." When I had a job, that was.

He looked across the desk and I shut up and let him finish.

"The late afternoons belong to the working man. We'd like them to stay later."

"So basically you want me to feed the customers bullshit to keep them here longer. You want them reaching into the cash machine to spend it on lap dances and booze." I figured that summed it up.

"Pretty much. Just don't lock the doors or firebomb the place to keep them inside." He looked up at me, studying. I couldn't tell if he was making a joke.

"Damn, Vince, don't even think that. I've about had enough for one day."

He unlocked a desk drawer and reached into it, withdrawing a wad of cash. He peeled off some bills and placed the money in an envelope. The man didn't take time to look at it or count it before handing it across the desk.

"There's about five hun there. Take some time to pick up a jacket and some shirts. Jeans are all right as long as they aren't greasy. Yes, you're a biker. Go figure. Get some shoes, too. I don't want you wandering around in sneakers or boots. The business crowd won't like seeing you in those. They'll think you're a customer left over from the last shift-change at the factory."

I didn't ask him what factory. "No problem. Thanks for the advance. Have you seen Tammi today?"

"No. Her shift doesn't start until nine. I don't keep track of the dancers beyond that."

I considered myself told. I patted the five in my pocket and headed out.

I shot all of Vince's advance on clothes and a pair of shoes. I kept the receipts and put them on his desk in case he wanted to check. It took about two minutes after I showed up for the women to begin flinging good-natured barbs in my direction. Word spread about the previous evening's food fest. Maybe my house rules didn't go unnoticed either.

Even DJ Ray got in on the act. Hell, the bouncers were in on it. With the ribbing coming from all sides, I held up my hands in mock surrender and found somewhere else to be.

I asked around for Tammi. No one had seen her. No big deal. I wasn't her keeper. She was probably off chewing the fat with some girls she knew. I kept an eye open for Danielle, too, but I didn't ask questions. I figured she worked a later shift. That, and I didn't want anyone knowing any secrets.

Hers, or mine.

I disappeared outside in the light of day to take a better look around the grounds of La Bonita. The building and the lot were in a hell of a lot better shape than what I had witnessed at El Diablo. Inside, new carpet covered the floor. The walls were clean and fresh-painted. Even the bar had a new top. Vince must have had the apartment done at the same time the construction crew updated the bar.

I wandered into the back and took a look at the private rooms. Low lighting and comfortable chairs dominated. I moved on to the restrooms. I knocked first, then called out. Nobody. Vince caught me backing out.

"From what I've seen so far, you're doing better than the last guy. I had to fire his ass."

That wasn't encouraging. "Fired? What for?"

"The bastard was useless. He pissed off all the girls, one at a time. I caught him stuffing coke up his nose with one of the dancers in the washroom. That was the end of both of them."

"I don't like what you're telling me about that. I'll keep my eyes open." No drugs. That was good. Nothing would tear people apart faster. It drew the worst and then some from what I could tell from my visit to the Diablo. I had no experience beyond that—at least that I would admit to.

It was late afternoon by the time I was satisfied with my look-see over the club. Tammi still wasn't around. If she was on-stage at 9—

Where the hell was that damned woman?

Tammi checked her buzzing phone. *Unknown number* showed on the screen. She answered anyway. She listened for a couple of seconds before her foot started a nervous tapping. The tapping lasted as long as the call. When it ended she was glad she picked up. El Diablo's bartender turned out to be worth the listen.

She clomped around the apartment, angry and frustrated that Frank didn't listen to her. She would have to do something after she got off work to ease the man's suspicions.

She dug out a thin white tee and a short skirt from her backpack. She tossed her bra and pulled the shirt on. She slipped a hand beneath it and squeezed a nipple while checking out her reflection in a mirror. Yes, it would definitely work. She reached down for her g-string and pulled it off to join the bra on the floor.

The apartment door opened and banged against the wall. He was here. She squeezed herself again, ran her hand under her skirt before dashing into the living room. She sat down and parted her legs to let him have a look. What the hell, he deserved it.

Startled, Tammi gasped and stood up when she caught sight of the man in her kitchen. "What are you doing here? You know he can walk in any second."

"I heard he was out at El Diablo asking questions."

"I already know. The bartender at the club called."

Fortunately, she got Frank to stop on the way to Fontana so she could let him know she was back in town.

"What are we going to do? If Frank finds out about us, we're in deep shit." Already Grant was looking panicked and antsy. She came to the conclusion she would have to exert more control over him.

"It's you I'm worried about." She remembered how the man checked out her breasts when she let him have a look back in Bombay Shores. "Frank doesn't have a clue. Just because he was asking questions doesn't mean he'll put it together." She needed to be right. Everything depended on Frank's continuing ignorance of what she was really going on.

"You'd better be right about that," Grant told her. "I don't want to have to deal with him after what he did to Jade."

"Come over here," she told him.

"Why?" He looked at her suspiciously.

"I'll show you when you get here." Grant was half-hard just from looking at her. That's what she liked about him. She ran a hand up the front of Grant's jeans and unbuckled his belt.

"What are you doing?"

Her fingers slipped over the hard-on beneath his jeans.

"That's what you get when you sit with your legs spread."

"In that case I'll do it more often. Let me finish you." She didn't let him refuse. She took him in her mouth and went to work. Grant grunted and started to come almost immediately. He allowed her to finish before he pushing her away and pulling up his pants.

"Next time I want something else."

She knew exactly what he wanted. She'd been putting him off for weeks. "I can't have you running out of the apartment when I'm trying to get Frank to forget about what he learned at El Diablo. He could see you."

"So that's why you're so agreeable."

If it took the promise of another blow job to get him to help her, it was a small price to pay. "Get out right now. He could show up any minute. And don't forget, you're coming back later."

She licked her lips. "We have a job to do." She lifted her shirt and aimed her breasts at him. "Double duty for you."

20

Tammi hoisted the heavy backpack from its hiding place and hauled it into the living room. She dropped it on the coffee table with a thud. The g-strings and tops and dresses she told Frank she packed back in Bombay shores were missing. She congratulated herself on being a good liar for making up the story on the spur of the moment.

She unzipped the backpack and reached in. It took both hands to pull out the five keys of plastic-wrapped coke. Who would have known just a short time ago she was broke and on her last legs? The bag would put her back in the money again. The ten pounds slipped from her sweaty hands and slammed onto the table.

Frank turned out to be a typical gullible accomplice. All she had to do was wind him up with a look at her in shorts and a tight t-shirt. Grant was the same way even when he was sleeping with Jade. Men. They were all the same.

Jade was right, though. Frank was well-hung and dumb. That woman was spoiled rotten by what Frank had dangling between his legs. She was looking forward to having her turn at being spoiled.

As much as she wanted Frank, as needy as she was, she had things to do. She tried putting him out of her mind, but it was hard. She smiled at the thought.

Tammi dug in the backpack for the scale. She cut into the package and scooped powder onto the coffee table for measuring. She went to work doing the same thing on the dining room table with a second scale. She covered the scale with paper, poured a measured amount onto it, and dumped the measure into plastic baggies.

The apartment door banged, startling her. She turned to see Grant storming in. The door slammed shut behind him. He halted in his tracks, taking in the woman bent over the table. She caught his eyes roaming. He reached for a bare thigh and started stroking. Not satisfied, his hand moved between her legs.

Tammi shifted away from the hand and made sure Grant was satisfied with another rub of bare thigh. She continued to pour powder from the scale into plastic bags. "It's about time you got here."

"You're getting fast at this, partner," Grant said.

"We better be. I don't want Frank stumbling in from his shift. He'll go ape-shit if he sees you."

When Grant didn't say anything, she debated whether she should tell him the truth about how Jade met her end in Bombay Shores at the hands of cartel sicarios. She decided against it. What the hell, it would keep Grant afraid of Frank, at least. It would allow her another measure of control over him. "Just don't forget how he left Jade. He'll take it out on both of us."

She finished with her part of the cut. All that remained was the residue on the table. She closed up and wrapped the coke and returned it to the backpack.

Jade's death wasn't the only ace she held in her game with Grant. There was one more thing she could use to keep him in line, something else he wanted so bad he could taste it.

"Grant."

He ignored her and kept on filling plastic bags. "What? I'm busy."

Tammi bent over the kitchen table. She pulled her dress up over her hips and aimed the part of her she knew he wanted more than anything in his direction.

"Grant!"

He straightened and caught sight of what she was offering. "Christ."

She pushed at her thong and it drifted past her thighs. She stepped out of it and spread her legs. She reached between them and rubbed.

Grant didn't want to give her time to change her mind again. He jumped the coffee table and leaned over her, pressing his hips urgently to hers. He made a grab for her top and yanked it down. His hands filled with firm, warm breasts. Somehow, he managed to separate his hands long enough to unzip his fly. He pushed his way deep into her center. There was no resistance.

"If Frank walks in now we're both dead, you bitch."

"Then hurry up and get it over with." Tammi's elbows collapsed as Grant's weight forced her onto the table. Bare breasts slipped into the leftover coke residue. It smeared her breasts. She rolled her hips, finishing Grant . She forced him down into the chair. She straddled him, making sure her breasts were at eye level.

White powder covered them. Grant licked, greedy for a taste of both. An erect nipple filled his mouth. "Damn you woman. You're going to be the death of me yet."

"Only if Frank finds out we knew each other back in Bombay Shores. He wouldn't be happy to learn he's running with a woman who split two ten-key parcels with his girl Jade."

"I don't think he was dumb enough to think Jade was his girl," Grant said.

"True. He was just holed up between her legs waiting out his bike parts." Men. Just like this one, they only wanted one thing.

"Yeah, and the way you spread your legs in a hurry for him makes me think you like him more than a little."

"He got me out of that dump I was living in, didn't he? I have to give him some credit for that. And don't you forget who was just between these legs, you jerk."

"That was nice and all, but I'd like to get between them from the front of you, not the back," Grant admitted.

"You'll have to take a number for that. Frank is number one right now."

"Right now?" he wondered. "Does that mean I'll get a shot?" He could hope, at least.

"Look between my legs. You just had your shot. And you're getting another one. Don't get greedy."

"You know what? You've got a funny way of being faithful to Frank."

She reached into the backpack and rubbed her hand in the coke. She got on her knees and wrapped her hand around Grant. He was nowhere near as big as Frank, but damn if he didn't taste pretty good with coke smeared all over him. She licked her lips. Grant grunted. She sucked and he was on his way.

"Shit. That was too fast."

He was quick in her mouth. She liked that. "Not for me. Now get the hell out. You got what you came for, and you came for what you got. Twice. I have to get back to work or there'll be hell to pay."

"If Frank finds out about us there'll be hell to pay all right. He'll kill both of us."

With Grant scared shitless of Frank, she needed to figure out a way to unload Grant and get Frank to take her farther north. It would be where the real money was. Then it came to her. "Wait a minute."

Grant was busy pulling up his pants.

"Not so fast. Take them off." Tammi got down on the floor on her back, legs spread, arms reaching. "I changed my mind."

Men were all alike. His mouth was open. He was practically drooling. His pants were already around his ankles. This would be easier than she thought.

She reached down to pull him against her stomach. She wrapped her legs around his back and squeezed. He could barely move. She felt the hardness against her belly. He was struggling, squirming. She almost gave in. She wanted it too. Then she remembered why she was on her back on the floor. "You're going to firebomb the club tonight," she announced. She was proud of herself for having come up with that idea.

"What?" Grant's needy squirming halted instantly.

"You heard me. You're going to firebomb the club."

He struggled to push off her. Her locked ankles kept him trapped. "How the hell am I going to do that? Dawg and Bull are out there all night. The lineup is half a block long."

She reached between her legs. She brought her hand up and rubbed it over the man's face. He sucked and licked at her fingers, hungry for the taste. She knew she had him. He couldn't refuse. "If you want more of that, you know what you have to do. Now get off me and do it. I don't care how."

Grant did as he was told. His hard-on was standing up against his stomach.

Christ but the man never got soft. She crawled over to him on hands and knees and took him in her mouth again.

His hips rocked back and forth, as though on automatic. "God damn you. You are a bitch."

"Shut up and let me finish. I like it when you come in my mouth."

She had him with that and she took him deep. He lost control and fell on top of her. She stayed attached. She liked showing him she was the boss. "There's more of this waiting for you when you do your job."

She got up and stood over him with her legs spread. Grant's eyes were caught between them. She reached down to wipe him off her thigh and rub it over her breasts. Transfixed, he could only watch. "You like what you see, don't you?"

Take a good look, you bastard. You're never going to see it again.

Nine o'clock came. Tammi's first shift of the night was beginning. I watched her halfheartedly as she strutted her stuff to her playlist and DJ Ray's performance. Ear-shattering whistles and clapping drowned out the music. Blinded by the spotlights, she would play up to the sounds of the eager audience and faces she could barely make out in the dimly lit room.

The front rows closest would leave the most money. I knew she didn't care if they threw it at her. The huge grin on her face wouldn't hurt either. Every man in the house thought she was smiling for him. Her tips would be good again tonight.

I spent a few minutes checking out the reaction from the crowd as Tammi picked up her routine. I never could figure out the link between a half-naked woman moving around on a stage and a hundred-dollar bill tucked into a g-string.

Especially when there was no chance the woman would end up going home with the former owner of the hundred bucks.

Sure there was always the lingering hope that someone would get lucky and get to take home one of the girls. In this club it was against house rules, but I knew it happened from time to time. Most of the performers never got involved with a client on a full-time basis. Quick cash was another matter. I was no strip-club first-timer. I knew how it was supposed to work—and how it really worked.

Sometimes a customer lived his dream and got lucky with one of the girls. Most of the time, not. If the girl was trying to make her way through university, she liked to have her regulars. If she got lucky, she could quit dancing and use her former regulars to pay her way through school. If she got really lucky, no one beat her up and she could keep away from the clubs until she graduated.

The unlucky ones got beat up. Got hooked on drugs. Ended up working for pimps who took all the money. It wasn't always a good life for a woman who turned dancing into hooking.

Sure, I was working the meet-and-greet, but it wasn't really my thing. I preferred to hang in the background, but I wasn't getting paid to do that. I walked onto the floor and moved table to table, working the crowd, trying to get to know the customers. The night crowd was definitely up-scale from the afternooners.

I went to let Dawg set me up at the door. He seemed to know almost everyone. With his help it wouldn't take long to get to know who the high rollers were. In a week I'd have it all down and I'd be able to relax.

A week. It had only been a day and already I was feeling like it had been a month. The ride out to El Diablo earlier knocked the wind out of my sails. It wasn't the ride that did that, though. The real kicker was what I learned while I was there.

My mind wasn't on work. I was thinking about Tammi. I knew this thing we had wasn't going to work out for either of us. Still, I was willing to give it a shot. It would be up to her how it shook out.

If she was doing drugs, or holding drugs, or selling drugs, I'd be disappearing in a hurry—this time, alone.

21

Tammi had no time to change out of her costume for the meet-up with Grant. She was running late and she needed to be quick to get back to the club. It was that, or suffer through Frank's questions—questions she didn't want to answer. Questions were the last thing she needed. That he was working in the same club she was dancing in became a liability overnight.

She slipped off her dancing shoes and hurried out of the dressing room to run barefoot to the apartment. The door was partway open. She cautiously eased it wider and looked in. When she saw who it was, she sighed with relief.

Grant was bent over the coffee table, busy cutting the coke. Judging by the residue of white surrounding the man's nose, he'd obviously been doing his share of taste-testing. If he couldn't keep his nose out of the product, what was the point of keeping him around?

"Did you have to? We don't have time for this shit. I need to collect what you've got and get back on stage."

He ignored her. She stood over him with her hands on her hips. Grant would have to go, the sooner the better. That she already made the decision made what came next easy. "You're stuffing our profits up your nose. Do you think that's a good idea?"

Grant handed over the baggies and she pushed them down the front of the shorts she'd hastily donned in the dressing room. "Good boy. Here's your reward." She undid her top and let him look. Christ, he was almost drooling. If it was one thing she knew, he wasn't going to be happy forever with only that. "You want a taste?"

She bent over to let him have a good look. Her breasts hovered in front of his face.

"I want more than a taste and you know it." He reached for her and she positioned herself on his lap. Her breasts were at just the right height. He rubbed his hand into what was left of the coke and spread it over both breasts. Her nipples rose to meet him.

"You are such a bastard." It was better he sucked up the leftovers than the good stuff.

"Shut the hell up and let me suck on them."

She leaned forward and Grant buried his face. He bit her, hard. She leaned back and slapped his face. Her nipple slipped from his teeth and she cried out in pain. He closed on her again. But for the nipple caught between the man's teeth she would have slapped him again.

"When you don't give me what I want, that's what you get."

"You had all you're getting for tonight. Now get out. Frank could come here looking for me." She glared at Grant for good measure. He shoved her off of his lap and almost ran for the door.

"Don't forget what you have to do if you want more of this." She stood up, turned around, and bent over, aiming what she knew he wanted more than anything else right at him. It looked like he was about to change his mind when she straightened, turned, and pulled up her top. Grant's loud groan pleased her. She smiled at him. "You know what you have to do. Next time you can have it all. Now get out of here if you know what's good for you."

She thought she heard the man whimper as he hurried through the door.

Even back in Bombay Shores, Grant had his problems with Tammi. He was addicted, no better than a common drug addict when it came to the woman. It was what she had between her legs that exerted control over him.

Having the woman on her back on the floor helped him over the edge. If she hadn't finished him with her mouth he would have slapped her silly and taken his good time with her. The bitch liked to think she could control men with what she had between her legs. He'd be showing her who the boss was soon enough. She was good at making promises. It was time for the woman to deliver if she knew what was good for her.

He had a bigger problem that needed solving now, though. He had to at least make an attempt to do what Tammi wanted. Firebombing the club. How had she come up with that? It was a crazy idea. With too many complications, as far as he was concerned.

There was always a lineup to get into La Bonita. How would he draw that lineup away from the front door? If he couldn't do that, he'd end up caught red-handed.

He tried to shut out thinking about how he was going to satisfy Tammi's demand. It came to him suddenly—a program he watched a couple of weeks ago. Something about magicians.

Then the light-bulb flashed and he knew how he'd do it. The bitch would finally see that he owned her when he completed his assignment.

Eager to comply with Tammi's request, he hurried home. He tipped the trash over, looking for some plastic and glass bottles. His neighbor's trash rewarded him with liquor and cola bottles. He retrieved a t-shirt from his bedroom and a pair of scissors. He drove to a gas station and filled the bottles before tearing the shirt and plugging the necks as tight as he could.

Grant's recon drive-by past La Bonita's front door told him what he needed to know. Groups of men, mixed couples, singles, stretched halfway down the block at the popular strip club. He would need a diversion to draw the lineup away from the front of the building. He needed to turn the crowd into lookie-loos.

He went past the club a second time before giving up. He parked at an all-night coffee shop and bought a stale donut and a cup of lukewarm coffee to wash it down. The bad taste it left in his mouth wasn't enough to distract him from his vision of Tammi on her back on the floor of the apartment. That woman would be the death of him yet if he wasn't careful.

Grant got back in his truck and drove past the club a third time, looking for something, anything, to make sparks fly. Then he saw it—a one-ton with a white tank in the bed. It would be too easy. He parked down the street and selected a gas-filled plastic bottle.

He climbed into the truck's bed and placed it on its side beneath the propane tank. He put a flame to the gas-soaked cloth jammed firmly into the neck. It caught instantly. He jumped onto the sidewalk and made for his own truck.

The plastic began to melt. In a few more minutes the spreading flames created by the fumes would produce enough heat to create a boom. If the ruse worked, noise and flame would draw the people lined up at the club and turn them into moths to be drawn to the orange glow of the burning propane tank.

Grant positioned his truck closer to the front door of La Bonita. He double-parked and waited. He was ready for a quick getaway if his plan went to shit.

Impatient for the action to begin, his eyes shifted from the front of the club to the mirror and the jury-rigged time bomb and then back to the club out his windshield.

An orange ball of flame engulfed the truck. The explosion shattered his rear window. The exploding propane tank flipped the truck into the street. It rolled onto its back and continued to burn as the escaping propane gas fed the flames.

The punctured gas tank added to the excitement, creating a second ball of flame. Orange sheets of glass reflected in store windows unbroken by the explosion.

The parade of people shifted from the entrance to the club and moved toward the disturbance. They all wanted a better look. Spectators streamed from the sidewalk into the street to watch the show.

It went better than he thought. Damn but Tammi was going to be proud. He put the truck in drive, kept his foot on the brake, and slowly eased it in the direction of the club's front entrance. He lit the gasoline-soaked cloth stuffed in the glass bottle. He held it out the window. As he drew across from the door, he tossed it. It bounced off the wood with a solid thud and shattered on the concrete steps.

The second bottle broke against the top of the wooden door. Gasoline ran down and ended up ignited by the flames from the first. He stopped the truck, got out, and flung the third bottle hard against the door. It too smashed to pieces, spreading gasoline to add to the flames already engulfing the huge wooden doors. He smiled, satisfied by the raging inferno he created, and got into the truck.

Grant didn't waste time standing around to watch. He jammed the gas pedal to the floor and peeled off in a cloud of smoke and squealing tires. *Highway to Hell* played on an oldies station.

He cranked up the volume and made for the freeway.

22

The club's wailing alarms didn't register on the noisy crowd immediately. DJ Ray was first to notice, only because of the alarm horn located directly above him in the loud club. He cocked his head and looked up at the blaring horn before turning down the music to check again.

On stage, a familiar dancer froze in her routine, as though she needed music to move at all. She looked over at Ray. He shrugged and looked up at the alarm. Impatient at the unscheduled halt in the show, the crowd began chanting. Raised fists waved encouragement for the dancer to carry on without the music.

In the relative quiet of the break in the action, a single high pitched voice yelled *Fire!* over the club's PA system. The voice got picked up and became a chant. It was only then that it slowly started to dawn on the patrons.

Alarms blared in every corner of the huge room. The noise level increased as people began yelling and screaming. Chairs toppled. Tables tipped. Bottles scattered on the carpeted floor. Men began scrambling toward the exits. They stumbled and tripped and fell and got up to do it all over again. Some crawled on their bellies in panicked attempts to make for the building exits.

Someone made it to the front door, only to be greeted by an orange wall of flame on the step. The door slammed shut, and was opened again. A second fireball flew into the club. It landed on the hard tile floor, bounced, and broke. Gasoline exploded and flames engulfed the carpet.

Another orange ball appeared out of nowhere. This time it was running through the club. In his haste, the running man almost made it past me. I braced. My chair tipped. I stuck out a foot. Arms that weren't mine flailed. Legs gave out and kicked and the man crashed to the floor.

There was too much fire to get close enough to attempt to roll the man over on the floor. I threw my jacket overtop and grabbed for a beer bottle. It came up empty. I made a grab for another and placed a finger over the mouth of a second. I shook them both as hard as I could.

It took what seemed like forever before the man went from funeral pyre to a mound of steaming beer fumes. The smoke and flame cleared and I recognized Bull. For good measure I sprayed him with two more bottles of beer. I guzzled half of the fourth and handed Bull his half.

"Frank. Holy shit. Thanks man. I thought I was a dead man. I owe you my life. Thanks."

"Show me your hands, Bull," I ordered him.

I took his shaking hands and did a quick examination, turning them over and over. They didn't look burned, but what the hell did I know? I spent all my spare time on a motorcycle. "Take off some of those clothes."

Bull stripped down to his skivvies. I made him turn around. "Christ, Bull, there's not a burn mark on you beyond a bit of pink skin on your hands."

Bull's eyes rolled in their sockets. He leaned on a table for support. "Shit. Shit. I saw it all. My whole life. All in slow motion. The minute I opened that damned door. I thought I was going to die."

"You'll be all right. When an ambulance gets here you need to get checked out."

Bull's entire body started shaking. I couldn't tell whether it was from fear or anger. "Screw the ambulance ride. I heard enough sirens when I was a kid growing up on the streets. I'm going out to look for the son of a bitch that doused me in gasoline. If you see Vince tell him I'm taking some time off."

"Bull, put your pants back on. I don't want it to be my fault when you're brought up in front of a judge on public indecency charges."

He had his shit together enough to snicker and I knew he was all right.

"I owe you my life. You ever need anything— anything—you come to Bull. You hear me, Frank?"

He shook my hand again before pulling on his pants. He borrowed my too-small jacket and hurried outside. If I knew anything about the man, he'd be busy keeping his word to look for whoever and whatever tried to kill him.

The ambulances were gone. The fire trucks too. In the quiet aftermath of the firebombing, I had time to think. It wasn't a coincidence. Since having one tossed at me on the freeway, I figured the second was another warning. I still had details to work out, but I had enough to put two and two together.

I couldn't prove Tammi and Jade were partners in the drug theft back in Bombay Shores. Instead, I figured on Buddy being the link to both of them. When Jade dumped him, he probably went to the cartel to save his ass. They sent him back to sniff around when they discovered what was missing.

At some point, Tammi must have told Buddy what Jade was holding in her closet. That's when he broke in to take a look for himself. Jade made sure I was there to scare him off—which is what she got when she made sure I moved in.

Buddy had to have reported back to his handlers. They sent out reinforcements in the form of the sicarios. Hit-men didn't hesitate to do what they had to do. It became their job to retrieve the missing drugs and send a message. The only way to do that was to kill the thief.

I knew why Tammi was trying to convince me to take her north. She wanted to get farther away from her pursuers. Then there was the side benefit. She would get a pile more money for what she was selling out of her backpack.

She didn't give a shit about me. I was only the means to an end. I thought I was the dumb one until Tammi started dancing in the club under her own name. She was so greedy and drug-addled she couldn't know it would give her away.

It was time to sit down with Tammi. If only I could find her. She had been avoiding me ever since I rode out for my visit to El Diablo. Already I could hear the recriminations flying around the room.

She'd accuse me of spying on her. She'd tell me all I had to do was ask. That she would have explained everything—even though she admitted she knew nothing about the freeway firebombing.

I was suckered into a relationship with another lying woman—the story of my life since I pulled up stakes and rode out of Mexico.

23

Tammi gyrated and bounced her way through her set with splits and slides and jumps. She cut her set short and strode back and forth across the stage in her haste to collect the cash on the stage floor. She was impatient to get it over with and get back to the apartment where she could confront Grant once again. She needed him to do what she wanted.

The fool was stuffing their product up his powder-covered nose faster than he could inhale it. He had to go, the sooner, the better as far as she was concerned. Her mind returned to her stage character. She concentrated her gaze on the reflection in the huge mirrors on the back wall. What little was left of her costume sparkled in the bright stage lights. She was so intent on Grant she didn't realize half of her costume was still covering her up.

She bent over slowly. Her hands hesitated at her g-string, teasing. The crowd hooted and cheered, anticipating what was to come. She hooked her thumbs beneath the straps on both hips, bent all the way down, and looked out over the crowd from the vee formed by her spread legs.

The cheering halted. Chairs tipped. Tables toppled. Panicked people scrambled for the exits. It took a moment before she realized there was no music. A blaring fire alarm replaced it. She straightened and kicked off her plastic shoes and ran to the back door. She heaved the heavy door open and made for the apartment. She almost toppled over Grant in the tiny kitchen. Already he had the backpack out from behind the living room sofa.

"What are you doing? The club is on fire."

Grant continued rolling the twenty. Satisfied with the result, he inspected it before bending over the counter. He stuffed one end of the roll into his nose and inhaled the three-line setup from the counter.

Tammi slammed the door. Grant almost jumped out of his skin. It occurred to him that perhaps he shouldn't have given up on making good his escape via the interstate after all.

"You can't keep your hands off of anything, can you?"

Panicked, he pushed back from the counter and circled Tammi, almost dancing in his eagerness. "I did it. I did it. Now you owe me. You fucking owe me."

"So I owe you. Why couldn't you wait until I was out of the club at least? When Bull ran in through the door covered in flames I thought I was going to get trapped in that dump."

"Screw Bull," Grant exclaimed. "You owe me. Get on your back. Get on your back, woman."

"Slow down. Rub yourself in some of that coke. You know how I like to suck you when you're covered in it." Tammi made a grab for Grant and pulled him into the living room. She pushed him down on the sofa and went down on her knees in front of him. Simpleton. He was even easier than Frank.

Grant grabbed her shoulders and pushed her hard onto the floor. Surprised by his eagerness, she fell and rolled onto her back. Her legs splayed in disarray. Her eyes locked onto something under the sofa. In that same instant Grant yanked the g-string past her ankles and pushed into her.

She didn't struggle. She had Grant where she wanted. The rest began falling into place fast. She rocked her hips and Grant grunted and emptied into her. She rolled onto her side and he slipped off.

"Happy now?"

"We're not done yet," he insisted.

"No, we're not."

Grant couldn't tear his eyes away.

"Get on your back. I want to ride you," she said.

Grant rolled onto his back. He glued his eyes to her breasts. He made a grab and watched her nipples harden. She reached for the table and rubbed her hand in what was left of the coke. She smeared it across her breasts and leaned over him. He buried his face between them and fastened his mouth to an erect nipple. She let him have all he wanted.

Grant was hard again. Jesus he felt good inside her. She knew already she was going to be fast. Without thinking, she reached underneath the edge of the sofa and made a grab for the drywall knife.

She brought it out and slipped the blade. Her nipple popped out of Grant's mouth and his eyes widened when he saw what she had in her hand.

Tammi gasped and screamed and lost control. She groaned and began to tremble. Her hips bucked. She screamed again and felt herself contracting. Grant grunted and squirted into her a second time. Mid-way through her own orgasm she tightened her grip on the knife. She bucked again and lost control a final time. The knife slashed at Grant's throat as her body heaved over him, again and again.

Grant didn't have a chance. He never uttered a sound.

Tammi's body convulsed again, still beyond her control. Finally, she leaned over and pushed herself off. She stayed crouched beside him, trying to breathe. Sweat and Grant's blood dripped onto the carpet.

She had no idea how long she stayed bent over Grant's limp body. It was all she could do to move. She tried to stand up. She couldn't. Instead she reached down to rub herself and her nipples hardened. If the son of a bitch wasn't limp she'd climb on top of him again.

She stayed on the floor, kneeling beside Grant's body, breathing, trying to catch her breath. Still trembling, she made another attempt and managed to push herself up off the floor. She reached for her phone and dialed 911. She grabbed a bed sheet, covered the table with it, and threw her backpack in the closet.

The banging on the door grew louder.

I was successful getting drunks and stragglers out of the club. Bull was gone, disappeared and headed for parts unknown. He had a close call and some luck that I had the presence of mind to get him on the ground and douse the flames. The fire trucks and ambulances were the last to depart.

A cop left the investigation and began asking questions. I told him what I could about the fire, but it was essentially nothing. I hadn't seen anything beyond the results of the gasoline bombs. Satisfied, he took a radio call and rushed off toward the alley and the rear of the club to the parking lot. He halted, looked around, and saw me as I was about to walk past him to the apartment.

"Is there something wrong?"

He gave me the once-over. "We had a report of a rape."

"What? A rape?"

"That's right. Why are you here?"

"I live here."

The cop opened the door. I managed a quick look as the officer entered the apartment. A male body lay sprawled on the floor in front of the sofa. His pants were down around his ankles. The man looked familiar. What the— Grant? What was he doing here?

I heard Tammi in the kitchen. She was sobbing her eyes out to someone, most likely a cop. I took another quick look through the doorway before another cop turned me around and chased me off. The sight of Tammi's knees and thighs, covered in blood, forced the hair on the back of my neck on end for the second time in a week.

How the hell did her legs get covered in blood?

Something wasn't right. I got smart and headed for the club. If the cops wanted to ask about Tammi's attacker, they could come and find me. A couple of hours later they tracked me down to fill me in on what happened in the apartment.

The officer said Grant was harassing Tammi. She tried to get away from him by coming to the city. It didn't work. Apparently, Grant's attempt to firebomb La Bonita had been part of the harassment. After he set the fire, he probably saw Tammi running from the club to the apartment. That was when he chased after her and attacked. She did the only thing she could when she saw the box-cutter. It appeared to be a case of self-defense.

Yeah. According to Tammi. Too bad Grant couldn't speak for himself.

The cop left, hoping for pastures greener than me. He began interviewing victims of the gasoline bomb thrown into the club. There were plenty left to work through. No one was allowed to leave.

I took time digesting what I was told. The more I thought about it, the more it didn't add up. The cops might not have any questions, but I had a few. It was Jade who was being harassed by Grant in Bombay Shores, not Tammi. Tammi was on the run from cartel killers. There were two fire bombings and a rape to Grant's credit.

Except I didn't believe the rape story. I was no cop, but it looked to me like Grant was on his back when his throat was slit. How were they going to explain that? And how had Tammi's knees and thighs gotten covered in blood?

This was turning into another Bombay Shores, but it was more complicated than that. Tammi was involved up to her ears this time. If she didn't get started digging herself out, she was going to end up like Jade.

I wasn't so anxious to share the grave.

24

The morning after the fire, Vince called in the staff to make an announcement. We all lingered by the stand-up bar, waiting to learn if or when the club would re-open. Speculation ran rampant. The fire department had shut us down. The police had shut us down. The city had pulled our permits and liquor licenses.

It didn't seem right, somehow. We all witnessed the damage limited to the outside of the entrance. That, and some scorched carpet in the club. Still, rumors flew among the groups surrounding the bar. The place was losing money. Insurance wouldn't pay. The fire was the last straw. It was another excuse to close up for good. Everyone would be laid off and sent packing without pay.

A smaller group at the end of the bar talked in subdued voices about Tammi and Grant. When they spotted me, they quieted.

Finally Vince climbed into DJ Ray's booth and the chatter halted. We waited to hear the man's marching orders for the club's opening. If it would open. Vince looked out over the group. Seemingly satisfied, the microphone squealed as he switched it on and began his announcements.

"As you saw when you walked in, damage is minimal. The door will be replaced. Fresh paint and new carpet will cover the scars. It's going to take more than a little fire to shut me, and all of you, down. Best of all, we're going to re-launch at nine p.m. tonight.

Applause and cheering echoed through the huge room, empty but for the employees.

Vince went on. "The police are working on the who and why. From what I've been told, it looks like it was random. Someone tried to make it personal when he took a liking to one of the dancers."

The quiet chatter among the group halted, replaced by an uncomfortable silence.

"Before you leave, there's one more thing. Take the rest of the day off and enjoy it. You'll all get paid as though you were at work. Come back tonight and we'll start the re-launch with a full shift and a whole new attitude."

As though to emphasize the news, contractors chose that moment to appear. They carried equipment into the club. Power tools and painting equipment appeared. When the employees spotted what was going on behind them, wild chants and applause brought the house down. The rush to the door left an empty room but for the construction workers. Vince waved me over to DJ Ray's booth. He was the last person I wanted to see, and sure as hell the last I wanted asking questions.

"Do you have any ideas about what happened last

night?" he asked.

Did I, or didn't I? Did I want to keep working here? Or was it time to hit the road and get far enough away that whatever was going on wouldn't be following me around for the foreseeable future?

"Grant was no stranger to me or to Tammi. I first ran into him in Bombay Shores."

I told Vince how I ended up with Tammi on the back of the bike. I re-hashed the firebombing attempt on the night we arrived. I told him again about riding out to El Diablo the next day and what I learned when I started asking questions about Tammi.

"I think Grant and Tammi were connected from the start. I don't think the club's firebombing was random. Someone had to put Grant up to it."

How, or who, I didn't know. It was obvious now that it wasn't healthy for anyone to be around either of them.

"Well, there's one less now. What do you think I should do?"

I thought about telling Vince to boot my ass and Tammi's out the door as fast as he could before the entire club ended up burned to the ground. Not wanting a club turned into a smoking pyre would make for a wise choice.

I didn't go with that.

"I don't know, Vince. If you want me to get her out of here, I'll go."

He looked at me, appraising, before his gaze returned to the burned-out door. "I know a guy. Let me pass everything on to him and we'll see what he comes up with."

We shook on it, but I knew my days at La Bonita

were numbered. If Vince was going to pay someone to look into Tammi's background, there's no telling what nightmares a real investigation would come up with.

Grant's sudden appearance wasn't random. He'd been around since Bombay Shores. How Grant managed to get into the apartment was anyone's guess. Tammi wasn't talking. Because of the police investigation, she said. Sure as shit there was more to it than that.

I went looking for Tammi, but as usual, she wasn't around. She must have thought she was better off making herself scarce before I came back to ask more questions she didn't want to hear. Even without her answers, I knew I didn't need another woman with a drug problem in my life.

The latest effort to set fire to the club was a crazed attempt to send another message. But who was the message for? Then a light bulb went off like a Molotov cocktail flung into the dark of night.

I hurried to the apartment, on the hunt for anything to confirm what was obviously staring me in the face. For my efforts I ended up finding a wad of cash tucked into the sofa. Either Tammi was making more in tips than she was telling me, or something else was going on that involved Grant, drugs and distribution.

I stashed the wad in a saddlebag and eased the bike out of the lot. I headed west past Beaumont and then Banning and the desert. On the way I contemplated life.

The firebombing. Grant's attack on Tammi and his subsequent death. Her past life at El Diablo. It was all catching up. It was time to re-evaluate.

What the hell was I doing? I already had a bellyful of Jade back in Bombay Shores. I narrowly escaped getting shot in the back. Now Tammi joined the pack. I was fed up with being played for a sucker.

I was better than that, and I knew it.

I backtracked to Banning and took the 243 and its twisties into the hills. By then it was late afternoon and I was mentally exhausted. Still plenty fed up, I reversed course and headed back to the city. I wasn't looking forward to confronting Tammi.

Before I knew it I was in front of the diner. I hated to admit it, but Danielle turned out to be foremost on my mind. Why I felt the need to share my dilemma with her, I didn't know. It was my lucky day when she came out to greet me, so I smiled. I could still do that, at least.

"I heard you ride up. What's going on?" she asked.

"Did you hear what happened at the club last night?"

"No. Yesterday was my day off. I've been working here. What happened?"

I would have started right in on the events of last night, until I caught a glimpse of the face she was shielding from me. It was covered in thick makeup. She didn't seem to me to be the type.

I positioned closer for a better look. She caught me examining her and turned away again. It was too late. Either the car she was riding in had to be a complete write-off or someone had taken a fist to her face.

"Never mind about the club," I told her." What happened to you? Will you tell me about it, or are you going to force me to be a gentleman and ignore it?"

Her face flushed through the makeup. To cover for

being caught out she poured me a cup of coffee and disappeared into the kitchen. I could hear whispering. When she came back she had on her street clothes. "Let's take a walk."

25

I was flabbergasted. "What happened to your face?" In the bright sunlight, it was easy to see past the makeup. Danielle didn't seem to be the makeup type, but she had it packed on pretty thick. I was quick to jump to conclusions. "Who put the fists to you?" I couldn't tell what her clothes were hiding.

"My boyfriend is the jealous type. I mean he was. He's not my boyfriend any more after what he did. He came home drunk last night. It seems someone at the club told him I was seeing somebody on the side."

Could this have been my fault? "I discovered this place and you completely by accident. I didn't say a word to anyone." I only hoped she believed me, because I hadn't breathed a word to anyone. Tammi, on the other hand, was the jealous type. I started to wonder if she had some connection to Danielle's boyfriend that neither of us knew about.

"Whether you did or didn't, it wouldn't matter to him. Someone said something. He's crazy jealous. He'd never let me ride to work at the club. He always dropped me off and picked me up when my shift was over."

"Do you think he might have seen us on our walk?"

"I don't know. I don't care any more. He's in jail. I hope he'll be cooling his heels for a while. With my luck he'll be out in a day."

"Is there anything I can do?" I still felt some measure of responsibility.

"No. Well, you can listen to me whine about it."

Taking a beating and talking about it didn't sound like whining to me. Hell, Danielle had to be tough as nails to take a shit-kicking and still be walking and talking. "I don't think it's whining."

She changed the subject, obviously embarrassed that I caught her out. "You were going to tell me about the club. What's going on?"

"I was, but first I want to know more about you and riding. Did I hear that right?"

"Don't hold out on me about the club. I'll tell you about the other later. What happened last night?"

There was no sense honey-coating it. Danielle would find out soon enough when she went in for her shift and found it closed. "The club was firebombed."

"What? Firebombed? As in a Molotov cocktail? Was anyone hurt?"

"You heard right. Bull had a narrow escape. I got to him in time. No burns, nothing. I sprayed him with a couple of bottles of beer."

"So he's all right then?"

I nodded. "Yup. Not even one bit of pink skin anywhere. I know, because I made him strip down in the middle of the club so I could take a look."

She looked relieved. "Do they know who did it?"

"Grant's truck was parked on the street. When the cops checked it out, they found a lighter and some rags and empty bottles. The thinking is that it was some form of revenge."

"Who's Grant?" Danielle wanted to know.

Shit, now I'd have to explain everything. "How much time do you have?"

"Eddy gave me the rest of the day off. I think he's taken a liking to you. I'm going to collect my riding gear. You can wait here for me."

I went in and poured my own coffee. Eddy fixed some sandwiches. He must have been eavesdropping. I didn't mind.

"Take these with you. Ham and cheese and lettuce on dark rye. She eats them all the time when she wants lunch."

"Do you know what happened to her last night?"

Eddy started in on an explanation before thinking better of it. He halted mid-sentence. "I think she should be the one to tell you about it if she hasn't already."

I nodded and took the sandwiches out to put in a saddlebag. The throaty exhaust of Danielle's pearl-white motorcycle pulled in next to my bagger. "Is that new, or do you wax it a lot? You do realize that the more time you spend washing and waxing, the less time you have to ride."

A huge smile crept over her face. In an instant it ended up a wince. Minus the makeup she washed off, not one but two of the blackest eyes I ever saw were visible behind the sunglasses. She had to be hurting a ton.

"Just because I have eyes like a raccoon doesn't mean I'm not willing to give you eyes to match at the slightest provocation." She made a fist but she didn't grin. It probably hurt too much.

"If you're expecting sympathy by bragging about your new look—"

"You're damned right I'm expecting sympathy," she interrupted. "What I want to know is, when is it going to start?"

"Right about now. Do you want to know where I'm taking you?"

"No. Let's just ride."

I grinned like a fox. "In that case, try to keep up."

I threaded us through traffic to the 215 and across to Hemet. From there I struck out on the 74. She didn't have any trouble keeping up. I led us to a lake and pulled off close to shore.

"You know how to treat a girl. I haven't been anywhere near here in ages."

"I wanted to see how you ride in the twisties. So far, you're doing pretty good for a girl." I grinned at her.

"And don't you ever forget about the girl part."

I looked across at her before getting off the bike. "There's no forgetting."

This time she didn't blush. "You were going to tell me about the club."

"In a bit. Eddy cooked one of your favorite meals when you weren't looking. You're going to sit and enjoy it or else. When you're finished, I'll get to it, but first I'm going to tell you a story."

"Oh great. Another man in my life with a sob story I'll be forced to listen to." She smiled. I didn't mind.

"This all started when I broke down by the Salton Sea."

"What were you doing there?" Danielle asked.

"It's my escape. I was on my way home after a winter down on the Baja. I like it there. The weather is great and the locals are friendly if you learn a bit of the language."

"I've never been, but it sounds like life on the Florida Keys."

I let her mention of the Keys slide, but I filed it away. "I needed a place to stay while I waited for parts. At the motel, I crossed paths with a woman who had room for me."

"Was that Tammi?"

"No. It was Jade. Tammi was a friend of hers."

"You get around with the women," she said.

"Sometimes." I hesitated.

"Don't stop now. I can take it."

"You enjoy giving a man a hard time, don't you?"

"Only the ones I think need it. Finish your story."

"I was mean to you when we first crossed paths at the diner. I'm sorry."

"I put it behind me and moved on that very day. Didn't you notice?"

How could I not like this one? I told her about the drugs and taking Tammi out of Bombay Shores. Then about El Diablo, and finally arriving at the Bonita. She asked about my arrangement with Tammi.

"We share the apartment below the club."

"What else do the two of you share?"

She must have that figured out by now. "Well, we sleep in the same bed if that tells you anything." There was no sense lying about it.

"Did I miss anything else last night?"

"Yeah, there is one more thing. Tammi was attacked and raped by Grant. I found out that was going on when I was trying to get everyone out of the club during the fire."

"I'm sorry to hear that. Is she all right?"

"Well, apart from dealing with cutting the guy up, she's fine. Grant, not so much. When the cops were looking into that, they discovered his truck parked by the club. They found glass bottles, rags and a lighter."

"Which means he was probably the arsonist," she said. "Did I just hear you right? Tammi knifed him?"

"I thought you missed that part. Yeah, she did. She slit his throat with a box knife while he was raping her."

"Holy shit. How is she handling that?"

"I don't know. She seems to have disappeared— and I don't think it's into therapy."

"What's happening with the club? Is the damage going to get fixed?"

"Vince closed the club for the investigation. The repair people showed up while he was in the middle of telling us it would open tonight at nine. I'm not sure if I want to keep working there now."

"It sounds like you have a decision to make, Frank."

"I think you might be right. Now let's hit the road. It'll be dark by the time we get back."

We rode together as far as the diner. Danielle waved when she turned off. I waved back and reluctantly rode on to La Bonita. I wasn't looking forward to spending another night under that roof.

Talking about it gave me a better picture of what

was going on. I was sharing my bed with a woman who used a box-cutter to slice a man's throat. Funny thing about that, though. When I got there, Grant was on his back in a pool of blood. There was no sign of a struggle. Tammi's knees were covered in blood.

When she did the cutting, either she was giving him a blow job or riding the daylights out of him.

Or maybe both.

Tammi was on me like a wet shirt the instant I walked in the door. One problem, though—she had on the clothes she was wearing last night. I looked hard, but I couldn't see even a spot of blood.

"Where the hell have you been? And what are you looking at? I waited for you in this dump all afternoon and you never showed."

She was a mess. Makeup washed down and smeared her tear-stained face. She had difficulty talking. Her words slurred. She was drunk or high or maybe both. "What can I say? I was out. I went for a ride." I wanted to ask about the cash stuffed in the sofa. She didn't give me the chance, and I wondered if she noticed it was gone.

"Were you out with that bitch again?"

Again? How could she know that?

"I know she's got a bike," she said.

Who was feeding her information? "For crying out loud, woman. I only just met the girl the other night in the club when she brought me a beer."

"You look at her like she's a virgin begging to get laid."

She wasn't far from right, but I wasn't going to admit it.

"And she brought you two beers. You tipped her twice."

What was the point? In her stupor there'd be no reasoning with the woman. She peeled off her shirt, pulled up her skirt and straddled me on the sofa. She shoved her breasts in my face and I started chewing. That seemed to take her mind off of Danielle. Mine, too. She pushed off, leaving a wet patch on my jeans. She settled on her knees and went to work on my belt.

"This is what I need." She had my pants down in a flash. I helped. What's a man good for if he can't help a woman get his pants down as fast as he could?

Tammi rolled onto her back and I climbed on. Her hips shifted and she reached around to show me the way. She crossed her ankles and locked her legs around me. She shuddered and grunted. Nails raked my back. Her hips bucked but she couldn't throw me off. She was hanging on too tight.

I held on just as tight.

Somehow she managed to work her way into the very spot Grant was in when she slit his throat. Someone had cut out the carpet and cleaned up the mess. At least she wasn't doing me in a pool of dried blood.

Her bucking matched my rhythm and I finished in her. The sucking sounds her insides made kept me hard. She grunted when she pushed me off and went down on me. She looked up at me with a twisted grin.

I never said a word. All of a sudden I knew I had to

get my ass out of town. I was beginning to feel like I was only a couple of short steps from turning bat-shit crazy, just like she was. When she climbed onto me and went full-bore I forgot all about leaving. Instead I let her have another screaming fit.

Screw it. Maybe I'd stay until something better came along.

Vince was one smart cookie when it came to advertising. He knew word of the firebombing would draw a crowd like none the club had ever experienced. He was keen to take advantage of it and kept La Bonita closed until the very last minute.

Management made it clear to the staff it would be all hands on deck. No one complained. They were happy for the tips they knew would pile up until end of shift. The club's entire staff was called in to handle the crowd of gawkers.

The lineup started building early in the evening. It stretched down the block. It was a boisterous crowd. They all wanted to be able to tell absent friends about their experience when they were finally admitted. It wouldn't be long before they would be turned into a crazy audience for the dancers when the doors opened. Dawg and Bull were instructed to use the wands at the door to screen out the troublemakers that always turned out for a night such as this.

"I'm surprised to see you showed up."

Danielle wasn't wearing makeup. Even in the dim light of the club her bruised face stood out. She looked scared, too.

"I didn't want to be here. Vince called me to come in."

"I don't blame you. Tonight is going to be a zoo."

"It's not that. My ex is outside in the lineup." I followed her to the door and we stuck our heads out. Danielle collapsed against me before withdrawing her head in a hurry. My arm went around her and she straightened. "He saw us."

Okay, so maybe doing that together wasn't so smart. "I'll warn Dawg and Bull. There's no sense pushing it."

"Please don't tell them anything about us. I don't want anyone to know I work at the diner."

"Don't worry. What's his name?"

"Jake. Greasy hair. Shiny jacket. Big."

"I'll tell the guys. They'll take care of him. They owe me big-time after last night."

Danielle left and I grabbed Bull and took him aside. I didn't want to create a commotion. I only had to tell him there could be a person in the lineup that might make problems for our re-launch. I pointed in Jake's direction and described him.

"We're using the wands tonight. We're not taking any chances on someone causing trouble with anything more than a fist."

I took a better look at Bull. "Hey man, did you get some new threads?"

The shit-eating grin plastered across his beefy face said yes. "Thanks to you. I owe you."

"In that case, keep an eye out for Jake and maybe we'll be even."

I kept mum about Danielle's predicament. I figured if she wanted Bull to know, she could tell him when he noticed the bruised face. I strolled down the long line of eager customers, pretending to count. It was an excuse to check out Jake. The man wasn't that big, but he was stocky and he looked mean. At the last minute I changed my mind about getting close to him in the dark. Instead, I went back to the club. At the door I turned for another look.

Either Jake had disappeared or he was using the lineup for cover.

La Bonita was open for an hour, maybe a little more. It was packed with eager customers. Waiters scrambled from the tables to the bar and back to fill orders. Outside, the line advanced at a snail's pace. The jostling and shoving wasn't letting up. Everyone wanted to be in front of someone else."

Vince made sure to stretch it out to milk the relaunch for every dollar it was worth. Normally the dancers would be on-stage shortly after opening. It wasn't happening like that tonight with the late opening. He made sure the beer flowed to help get the impatient crowd worked into a fever pitch.

So far, Vince's strategy worked—that is, until it got close to the time for the headliner. DJ Ray had Tammi's playlist blaring over the speakers. The buzz from the crowd almost overpowered the sound system. Clapping in unison and chanting Tammi's name, the crowd demanded satisfaction.

I already knew Tammi was an emotional mess because of what happened, but she had to go on. There was no way she could say no. The lights dimmed and blinked, the signal for a dancer to appear on-stage.

I spotted her in the shadows on the edge of the

stage, out of the lights. Someone in the audience caught sight and pointed and the pandemonium began all over. The yelling and screaming intensified.

The lights came up. That was her cue to walk to center stage. She didn't quite complete the journey. She stumbled, caught herself, and fell. Her legs splayed. Her feet kicked. A dance shoe flipped into the audience.

The yelling and whistling stopped short, but the crowd gave her the benefit of the doubt. They were there to watch the star attraction perform.

Tammi managed to get up. Minus a shoe, her uneven gait caused her to trip. She went down again. She made a grab for the pole to steady herself. She leaned against it for support, regained her balance and kicked off the offending shoe.

Her sad performance wasn't pretty to watch. Neither was she.

The harsh overhead stage lights flipped on, revealing makeup smeared across Tammi's face. Her hair was a straggly mess. She must have thought naked was the new costume because she wasn't wearing one. She tried one more time to use the pole to pull herself upright onto her feet.

The strategy didn't work and she fell for the last time. She kept trying, like an insect on its back. She couldn't manage to coordinate her arms and legs. She was too high to know enough to give up. She didn't appear to have a clue where she was.

Cheers turned into jeers. Boos and catcalls drowned out the music. A bottle smashed against the pole. Beer splashed and drenched the floor. Not wanting her to be hurt, I forced my way through the packed crowd, climbed the stage, and picked her up. I carried her off. She passed out, dead weight in my arms.

Out of sight, I threw her over my shoulder and hauled her bare ass to the apartment. She cried and mumbled and shrieked and kicked the whole time. She screamed Grant's name. She said she was sorry. She mumbled more crazy shit I couldn't understand and then went back to shouting for Grant.

At least now I knew how Grant met his end. The drug-addled, crazy bitch killed him. I filed the information away after dropping her on the bed and went back to work.

Tammi's disastrous performance pretty much kicked the fun out of the night for me. The let-down didn't last long for the rest of the staff. The saving grace was the ever-changing, raucous crowd that tipped well all night. Once witnesses to the disaster were outnumbered by fresh faces in the crowd, things returned to the low boil that was brewing since the club's doors opened.

The night's turnout overwhelmed everyone. The attitude of the raucous crowd spilled over to the staff. Occasionally, I would cross paths with Danielle in the crowded bar, but we had no time for small talk. Still, I made sure I took my break when she did.

"I've been here for three months and I've never seen anything like this," she said.

"This is what you get when local news picks up on a story and runs with it. Everyone wants in on the show."

"I saw you going to Tammi's rescue. What kind of shape is she in?"

"She's out of it," I told her. "She couldn't move a muscle."

"She's going to wake up with a king-size hangover."

"When she wakes up she'll want something to stuff up her nose to get over the hangover," I corrected her. "I don't want to be around to witness that."

"So you've made up your mind?"

"Pretty much. I've had enough. A thousand miles of two-lane blacktop in a day wouldn't exhaust me as much as what's been going on."

"I don't envy what you've been through."

"When it starts to feel like its time to go, it usually is." I couldn't deny that.

"Is that the voice of experience talking?"

"I think we've talked enough about me. I want to know about you."

"How much time have you got?"

"About five minutes until break is over," I warned her.

"In that case, I'll give you the short version. I was brought up on the Florida Keys—born and raised. Because of that, I'm known as a conch." Danielle made sure to spell it for me and then said it again it before going on. "My parents run a small family-owned dive shop and sport fishing business. When I was little I worked behind the counter. When I got older I couldn't wait to get out, and here I am."

"I spent time riding the Keys back a few years. I've always thought I'd like to go back." I didn't tell her I wasn't in a hurry to get there. Life was too boring— which wasn't the case now. Maybe I did need more time on the Keys after all.

"My parents want me to take over the business. I'm not sure I'm ready. I don't think it's time to have that back in my life yet."

"I can't wait to hear the long version," I told her.

She smiled. "Well, you're going to have to wait. I need to get back to work."

27

The lights flickered and then dimmed, announcing last call. The hard-cores ordered another drink, but the dancers were long departed. There was nothing to entertain the stragglers beyond their last drinks. Tabs were finalized and paid, and it was bottoms-up and out. Twenty minutes after last call, those remaining were ushered out the door. Behind them, the doors were closed and locked. The only people left were employees cashing out.

Danielle was among the last.

"How did you do?"

"Just like everyone else. My pockets are full."

I let her know I set Bull on her ex. She didn't look happy to find out. I made sure to tell her I hadn't mentioned a word about us. "Your Jake disappeared when he found out we were using the wands."

"Thanks, but he's not mine any more. I'm glad he didn't try to get in, but chances are he didn't up and disappear. I'm too tired to think about it now. I'm heading home."

"If it's all right with you I'll be coming by for coffee in the morning," I told her.

"I'd like that, but don't let it go to your head. And don't be a smart ass—you know which head."

"You're just harsh, woman," I said, but I smiled.

"You know it. Good night."

I turned and almost knocked Tammi over. The last time I saw her, I was tucking her into bed. She was out of it and almost dead going by how she looked. No such luck. "How long have you been standing there?"

She was pale-faced and shaking like a leaf. "Long enough to know you've got the hots for that skanky bitch. I thought I told you to leave her out of it. Get rid of her, or I'll get rid of her for you."

So she had been the one to inform on me with Danielle's ex. "What is it with you? I haven't laid a finger on the woman."

"You better not have laid anything else on her either, if you know what's good for you. Now get your ass in gear. I'm tired and I want to go to bed."

The woman was so out of it she barely knew her own name. She made a grab for my belt and yanked me toward the exit. I couldn't tell whether she needed to hang on to steady herself or if she was eager to get me home and away from temptation. In any case, she was too late. I stopped short and detached her hand.

"Stay." I could be a son of a bitch too.

Tammi crossed her arms and tapped a still-bare foot. The stink-eye she aimed in Danielle's direction wasn't pretty. Why was she back in the club?

The woman didn't let up. "It looks like you got what you deserved. Your new face is an improvement," she told Danielle.

Danielle wasn't about coming down to Tammi's level. Her crestfallen look said something else was wrong. "What's up?" I asked.

"I've got two flat tires. This was stuck in the seat."

My eyes widened at the sight of the large version of a k-bar clutched in her hand. Her ex left a calling card.

"Too bad it wasn't stuck in your back, bitch." Tammi wanted a cat-fight. The hate-filled look told me I'd be wise to get one of them out of the place. I knew exactly which one, too, but Tammi wouldn't be liking it.

"I'll help you push your bike into the back," I told Danielle. "How are you planning on getting home?"

"I'll take a cab."

"No you won't. Grab your helmet. I'll take you."

Tammi's jaw dropped. Her foot stopped mid-tap. She waved her arms and stomped off to the back of the club and the dressing room. I didn't care any more. The writing was on the wall. Was I smart enough to read it?

I accompanied Danielle out to my bagger in the parking lot. I tipped it up and waited while she climbed on the back. She sat so light I could barely tell she was there.

"Just remember, woman. I'm driving this rig. No leaning into the corners," I joked.

"Yes, master."

"Okay, now I know you're screwing with me."

"Maybe. Maybe not."

"Refresh my memory. Who was it told me she didn't ride bitch?"

She punched my shoulder. "You're my first, but don't let your imagination run wild."

Damned if I could read this one. We rode the rest of

the way in silence until we got to her door.

"Do you want to come in?" Danielle asked.

Yes, I did, but that's not what I said. "I don't want to start a war with you two back at the club. Can I get a rain check?" For once, I said no. At least, it sounded like it. That was a new one on me.

"I don't give rain checks, either," she said.

"Seeing as how we just shot down the not riding bitch speech you laid on me the other day, I'll take a wait-and-see attitude."

"If you're going to give me attitude, your head is going to be monumentally sore by the time I'm finished with you."

I figured I should shut up, and fast. I didn't want to dig the hole any deeper than it already was.

Despite the promises I made to the contrary, I rode back to La Bonita and Tammi. I couldn't escape either one. Tammi and the club had a hold on me I couldn't break, no matter how many times the voice in my head told me to keep on going.

I took it slowly and gave myself time to think. How many times had I done just that in the last couple of days?

Would I remain in this sweet mess, or would I hit the road and get out of Dodge? There was no way I wanted to get into something with a third woman I didn't know. Hell, at the rate I was going, I'd be three for three by sunup.

Grant's death wasn't resting easy on my mind. Tammi creeped me out when she started mumbling apologies for killing him while I had her slung over my shoulder. In her drugged-out state, she didn't know what she was saying, but I was paying attention.

Women. Since leaving Mexico, two had been liars. One of them was a self-confessed killer. Yet I believed every story they handed off. If I was a rich man, I'd be broke by now. As it was, I was broke anyway—well, except for the wad stashed in my saddlebag. I'd almost forgotten about the cash I discovered stuffed into the sofa.

So far, Tammi hadn't missed it—not surprising in her drug-induced stupor.

La Bonita's neon came into view and I was ready to collapse and sleep the sleep of the dead. I parked and made for the apartment. What greeted me when I opened the door wasn't a pretty picture.

The living room was completely trashed. Tammi was knee-deep and thrashing around in everything she had thrown on the floor or smashed against a wall. I grabbed her wrists and forced her onto her knees. On the way down she made a feeble attempt at a kick but her legs gave out.

"That must have been quite a fit. Are you done now?"

She fell to the floor on her back with a whimper. Her temper tantrum was over. She was exhausted. "I will be when I get you between my legs."

Okay, so maybe she wasn't as exhausted as she led me to believe.

"If that bitch had you between hers you're going to be sorry."

I was already sorry, and the bitch she was talking about had only smiled at me. The trouble with Tammi was she couldn't let go of anything.

I picked her up. She passed out the minute I dumped her on the bed. I wouldn't have to deal with her drug-induced jealousy over a woman I only smiled at. Somehow, I didn't think Danielle was looking to hook up with the likes of someone like me after dumping the loser she was dating.

Come daylight, Tammi had me wide awake listening to her screams in the bedroom. I figured she had to be yelling into a phone to some poor son of a bitch behind the closed door. I crawled off the sofa and she hung up. She must have been keeping her other ear on me. "Who was that?" I asked.

"A friend. He heard about the rape and wanted to know if I was all right." Red-rimmed eyes, dilated pupils and disheveled hair gave her a wild look. Unkempt, greasy hair framed a face covered in a sweaty sheen.

One look told me what she was about. "You're using."

"I'm not using. I cried myself to sleep last night. I'm upset with what's going on between you and Danielle. The two of you seem awfully friendly all of a sudden."

I looked around the trashed apartment. Cried herself to sleep? Christ, she was barely breathing when I put her to bed. She was so tired she couldn't even snore. This one could bullshit with the best of them. "So all this was because of jealousy?"

"Yes, it's because of jealousy. Now can we stop talking about it?"

"We can stop, but it's not going to go away." I knew it would never go away for me until I left everything a long way behind. Tammi refused to let up.

"We need to get away from here. I know some

people at a club in Seattle. They're willing to give us a fresh start. We could head up there first thing."

I already knew the answer. I asked the question anyway. "Shit, that's almost in Canada. Why there?"

The farther north she could get would see her move whatever quantity of product she hadn't stuffed up her own nose. The value of the drugs would quadruple, at least. Two thousand dollars for a key in South America could wring two hundred-thousand out of needy people in the north. The trouble with that was when the seller was a user. It never ended in a good way.

"L.A. hasn't been good for us. This city is a jinx. We've only been here a couple of days and look what happened."

Fast talker that she was, she was right about that. Although, I just showed up and already I had an apartment, a job and a paycheck. It didn't seem like the jinx was on me if I took Tammi out of the equation. All I wanted to do was to last until payday. The way things were going, I didn't think I'd be around much past yesterday. Maybe I should admit I was jinxed after all.

"Are you coming to bed now? I'm tired."

Tired? Christ, she didn't even know it was already tomorrow. Tammi was wound so tight sleep was the last thing she was going to get. Added to that, I was starting to get a little shy about closing my eyes when she was around.

Some deep-seated need to help a woman in trouble willingly caught me up in Tammi's web. I ended up getting out of Bombay Shores with a reformed junkie riding bitch. All the bitch wanted was someone to help her move drugs.

Keeping her happy would be easy. All I had to do was stay on the move. When the drugs ran out, it was anyone's guess as to how I'd end up.

What I didn't want was to end up like Grant.

28

Tammi reached for me beneath the covers, impatient and eager. Her lips fastened onto me and I became just as eager. She moved up and her swollen nipples brushed against the length of me. I moved to climb over her. She cried out and pushed me back down before climbing on top. The length of me ended up between her legs in one long, fast downward plunge.

I didn't move. I didn't have to. She shuddered once and fell onto me, panting into my ear.

"You were quick."

"I needed it. I'll look after you when I catch my breath."

I moved to lie beside her.

"Don't. Stay in me. I need you there." She shuddered again and screamed.

All right, then. Officially, I was now borderline crazy, too.

Tammi's breathing became even. I nudged her to be sure. It was now or never. I got out of bed and went through the room. Nothing. In the living room I checked the sofa for more loose change. I moved to the bedroom. Bed. Mattress. Closet. Floor.

She slept through it all.

Her backpack leaned against the wall on her side of the bed. Could it be that obvious? I pulled a zipper and checked inside.

Oh yes it could. Where had I seen this before?

I pulled a package out of Tammi's backpack. Another scorpion meant another five-key block—or what was left of it. The second bundle of Jade's dope found its way into Tammi's backpack. I now knew why the woman was so protective of the damned thing.

At least this time there was no one holding a gun to my back—yet.

I dressed and threw what I could find on short notice into my pack. No way did I want to experience a repeat of what happened in Bombay Shores. In minutes I was out the door and pushing my ride down the driveway. I punched the starter and the bike roared to life.

I knew exactly where I was headed. I didn't try to bullshit myself. I almost made it, too, until flashing red and blue lights bounced off windows and fire trucks. Cops directed what traffic there was around the closed street. I parked and walked the rest of the way.

Orange flames and sparks illuminated a cloud of smoke drifting up into the night. Danielle and Eddy huddled together, staring into the ruins of what remained of the diner. I had no reason to think it had been torched, but my first thought was of Grant. Then

I remembered he was beyond this. Tammi was passed out in my bed so she was off the hook.

"Were you inside when it went up?"

Eddy looked at me and shook his head. "No. I got the call. Danielle heard the sirens and walked over to see what the fuss was about."

"I'm sorry, Eddy."

"That's it, you two. I've had enough. I'm done. The insurance will pay out and I'm moving to the Keys."

"What happened?"

"I don't know," Eddy said. "It was almost to the ground by the time I got here. The chief says it went up quick. He thinks something must have been used to get it going that fast."

"So someone set it on fire."

"It looks that way."

Danielle looked at me and I knew exactly what she was thinking. "It wasn't Tammi. I was with her."

"Then I can only think of one other person," she said.

I knew who that was. I had it figured Jake was the person on the other end of the phone with Tammi. He was taking the abuse, and I was pretty sure it was something to do with another bonfire. "Your ex."

"Yes. He won't be satisfied until he runs me out of town."

"Where will you go?" I wanted to know.

"I didn't say I was leaving. Now come on. We're going over to my place. Come on, Eddy. There's safety in numbers."

We sat around Danielle's kitchen drinking coffee. To kill time and thoughts of Eddy's destroyed dream, we made a game out of who could tell the saddest story.

So far, Eddy was winning. Danielle was a close second with her swollen black eyes. I didn't even consider entering the contest.

Danielle finally recalled Eddy's comment about the Keys. "What's this you were saying about moving? You never told me anything about a retirement plan."

"For the last few years I've been thinking about getting out of this town," Eddy said. "The traffic, the pollution, the politics are all wearing me down. I think when the insurance comes through I'm done and gone."

"The Keys, Eddy," she reminded him. "Don't change the subject."

"It's been a long-time dream of mine that this California boy should one day escape the big city and retreat to the laid-back Florida Keys. I've been thinking about the white sand and clear-blue water for a few years. I hear there's no polluted air down there."

"So that's the reason for the postcard pinned over the grill."

"Now you know."

In another life I rode in Florida. I gave up because I couldn't depend on the weather in the winter. "I've ridden down that way. There's plenty of places to get lost off the causeway. I think I'd like to go back there one day myself."

"You two are definitely a couple of dreamers. You both need to stop talking and start doing," Eddy said.

"I've had just about enough of being taken advantage of. I've been played for a sucker long enough."

"Danielle told me about your situation. I don't envy you one bit for what's been going on between you and that dancer."

"I tossed the place earlier tonight while Tammi was sleeping. I found what was left of a five-key block—again. Every time I open a door there's dope behind it—and I don't mean me."

Eddy grinned. "I don't know, Frank. Two for two is a pretty good average."

He was right about that. My only response was to grin.

"Not any more. My bag is packed and I'm ready to roll. All I have to do is stop in and tell Vince I won't be around. I'll pay back the five bills he loaned me and I'm good to go."

"Where will you get the money?"

As far as Danielle knew, I was broke. "I'll tell you later. I know you won't go along with it."

Eddie pushed back his chair and stood up. "Well, kids, I've had about enough. I'm going home. If you're ever in the Keys, look me up. I'll be in the book."

He hugged Danielle and shook my hand. "So long, Eddy."

It felt good to finally make up my mind while sitting in Danielle's kitchen.

"I'll let you stay for a little while."

She granted my silent wish. "So then, the decision isn't up to me?"

"That's right. I'll be throwing your sorry ass out at a moment's notice."

"I think Eddy has the sorriest ass around these parts, but I'll take what little sympathy I can get."

"While you do that, I'm going to take a shower. I won't be long."

She left the door open. I made no secret of looking.

With the light behind her I couldn't quite make out everything. From what I could see reflected in the mirror, she had it going on in all the right places.

"Are you coming?" she asked.

I hesitated. That was a first for me.

"Are you coming or not?"

Obviously I needed to be asked twice. "Yes. Sorry. I was busy looking."

"I know. I wanted you to," she admitted.

I undressed under her watchful eye. Hell, she was almost as bad as I was.

"Come closer."

I stepped out of my jeans into the running water. She turned to face me. She didn't look up.

"Hey, you.

She didn't answer. Instead, she cupped me in both hands.

"I'm going to like this. A hand snaked behind to force me closer. Finally, she looked up. "I need to try this on for size."

She sunk to her knees and her mouth surrounded me. She got busy, slowly at first. She wasn't new at it. I couldn't hold back, whether because she was greedy or I was willing, or both. I spilled out of her mouth and ran down onto her breasts. I pulled her up and kissed her.

"My goodness."

"What?"

"No one has ever done that before."

"If you want to wash off, the water's getting cold."

"I don't care. I'll wash it off later. Do you have any left?"

"Let's find out," I said.

Danielle took my hand and led me toward the bedroom. Without a word she got on her back. I leaned over her and moved my knees to surround her hips. I eased in, slowly. We shifted and she brought her feet off the bed and wrapped her legs around me.

"You fill me up." Her hand snaked around to cradle me. "Reach back and feel the wet.

My hand covered hers in the sea running out of her onto the bed. She giggled and shifted and even more seeped out.

"There's going to be a lot more of that in a bit."

"Yes.

I moved my head down to get to her nipples.

"Be careful. Not too hard. They're tender."

There was something I needed to remember about that, but damned if I was going to try now. She started milking me, pulling and gently squeezing. Her legs moved higher on my back and her hips pushed up against me. I kept my weight off her to allow her to move the way she wanted.

"I'm getting close."

"I'll wait until you're finished."

"Yes. Yes. Oh. Yes."

She bit into my shoulder and struggled to lift me with her hips.

"Now you. You."

Her hand went back to me and I was on my way. She forced every drop into her, running her fingers up to force it out of me.

"Oh God, we're a mess. Here, feel."

She took my hand again and held it against both of us.

"If that's any sign of what you've taken out of me,

I'm going to be empty for a week."

"I'm sore, but it's a good sore. My stomach and hips are all achy. I need a pillow."

"You do remember that you were supposed to be throwing me out sooner rather than later."

"So you're blaming me for this?"

"Well, yes. That's a man's job, isn't it?"

"If it is, you've sure done it. Now I just want to lie here like a lump and enjoy what we just accomplished."

"I'm not leaving."

"Yes you are. You're going back to the club to do at least two things. One, you're going to pay back Vince. Two, you're ending it with Tammi. If there's a third, I'll leave it up to you."

I liked number three the best. No pressure.

29

Damn but I had made some huge mistakes. I never learned. If I did, it was the hard way. I was in the middle of it all over again, this time, waking up in Danielle's well-made bed. Would she turn out to be a different kind of problem, or more of the same?

What the hell was I doing, and where the hell was I going with all of it? I'd trusted Jade until I discovered the five keys of cartel coca stashed in her closet.

I hauled her friend Tammi—who turned out to be a reformed junkie not so reformed—out of that mess and got us both lost in El Lay's bright lights. That didn't last long.

Both women turned out to be small-scale chapulínes, grasshoppers, going from place to place looking for customers. Except, they were selling stolen cartel drugs. Not a good place to be these days.

I turned to face Danielle. She looked at me, waiting. "You know, I was only trying to do that woman a favor. I figured on getting her out of Bombay Shores and away from whatever was going on with her friend Jade." I was looking for sympathy, but I knew I wouldn't get much at this stage.

"Yes, but you tried to settle her down—and you with her. She isn't ready for that. By the sound of it, she's tweaking, too."

I got it, but it only made me feel guilty as hell. "I think she's doing more than tweaking. What the hell am I supposed to do? I'm not her savior." I had that figured out, at least.

"What do you mean, more than tweaking?" How could she know? She couldn't. Should I tell her? "Well—" I hesitated.

"Don't hold back now. It's too late for that."

She shifted beneath the sheet and slid away, waiting for me to go on. It was too late. Wasn't I already in this one's bed? "She's selling." But that wasn't the main thing.

"So she's selling. Plenty do that with no problem."

While it was good to know Danielle didn't have a problem with a little selling on the side, I knew once I told her how much product Tammi had in her backpack, she wouldn't like it. "She's been unloading as much of a five key package of coca as she can at the club. Coca belonging to the Sinaloa cartel."

"How do you know that?"

Here we go. "Because of the picture of the nice scorpion glued to the package."

Danielle threw the sheet off and sat up. I couldn't help admiring her body. It was one that could take a lot of admiring and not get stale. I started to grin.

"What are you grinning at? You're shacked up with a woman selling stolen cartel coke. It's nothing to joke about."

"Yeah. No. I'm smiling at you naked beside me."

"You won't be smiling so much with your various body parts in a shallow desert hole in the ground. The coyotes will be gathering round and howling over the fresh meat."

Cut up and parted out. I'd heard about that. I didn't much like the picture she painted. "Maybe you're right and getting out of town is the thing to do."

Maybe? There was no doubt now, and I knew it. Still— "Before I allowed myself to get trapped in all of this my plan was to head home. Now I feel like going in an entirely different direction.

"Maybe it's time to go east," Danielle said.

"I'm too tired to think about it now. Is it all right if I stay here tonight?"

"You already know the answer to that," she said.

I slept like a dog except for the one time I woke up. There was a softly snoring woman in her bed beside me. Now we were in the kitchen, and I had the counter between us. Danielle busied herself with breakfast. "Has anyone ever told you that you snore?"

Danielle moved into the fighting stance she had in the diner when she smacked the back of my head. "I do not."

"Okay, maybe it's not snoring, exactly." I knew when to change the subject. "Something smells good. Are you making me breakfast?" Sometimes the obvious is the only way to a win.

"Breakfast? You should be so lucky. I turned the oven on. We'll see what comes out in a few minutes."

"Is it all right if I take a shower?"

"I'll get us a towel."

"No you don't. You stay right here. I like my women in the kitchen full-time. And barefoot, too." I had a shit-eater on my face so big I thought I'd topple over.

"The only thing missing from that is the pregnant part. Don't even think about it."

"I need to do some thinking and I can't think straight when we're in the shower together—in case you didn't notice last night." Damned if she wasn't grinning right back at me. I went in and turned the water on full cold and took my time.

At least Jade had been smart enough to keep her nose clean. It was obvious Tammi had hers shoved so deep into the product she could barely draw a breath without the coke going straight up her nose. She was a doper. Even I couldn't deny that.

She must have been fresh out of rehab when we met in Bombay Shores. Twenty-eight days wasn't enough. At this stage, I didn't think there would be a rehab that would be long enough.

Grant couldn't have realized what he was getting into when he got tangled up with Tammi. His death was unfortunate. Jade might have thrown his ass out into the street, but it was Tammi who killed him when his usefulness to her ended.

I knew what I had to do. It was staring me in the face since I rode to check out El Diablo. I got answers to the questions I asked, all right. I just didn't want to hear them.

Danielle brought me out of my reverie.

"I brought your bag in. It's by the door. You really did pack up last night. At first I thought you were handing me a line."

"No, I'm past that now. I'm too exhausted to lie. In fact, I may never lie to you—and that's not a good thing for a man to tell a woman."

Danielle gave me a quizzical look, and I knew enough to change the subject. "How are you feeling this morning?"

"What do you mean?"

"Last night you told me you were sore and tender."

"I feel really good. That pillow under my hips did the trick. My breasts are back to normal and I'm only a bit sore. Now stop asking questions. Sit down. Shut up. Eat."

"Yes, ma'am. So then, you can cook?"

She gently patted the back of my head.

I almost winced before teasing her. "Damn you, woman. That's twice."

"Give me half a chance and there'll most likely be a third."

"We'll just have to see about that."

I cleaned up the scrambled eggs and toast in record time. To show I wasn't a complete pig, I cleared the table and put the dishes in the sink.

"So tell me, who trained you?"

"There was one or two," I said.

"More like three or four if I know you." There'd be no messing with this one. It was my turn to gently smack her on the back of the head. "Tit for tat."

Danielle's smile turned serious. "You were a long time washing away your sins in the shower. What did you decide?"

"I've had a bellyful. I'm out. I'll ride over to the club and pay Vince what I owe him, and then I'm gone."

"I thought you were broke. I don't mean to pry, but where did you get the money?"

I knew she meant to pry. What woman wouldn't when a confessed broke-ass biker came up with a large sum of cash? "I discovered it sticking out from under a sofa cushion in the apartment. Call me a thief if you want, but it's staying in my pocket, just like the tips you talked me out of."

"It's none of my business."

I needed to hear that. "I don't owe that woman anything. I helped her get away from one problem and she put both of us right back into one even worse. For some reason I was too naïve to realize what the hell was going on. Call me a sucker, but the cash is mine. I'm keeping it."

Was I convincing myself, or was I trying to convince Danielle?

I had crossed the border only a week ago. It felt like one hell of a lot longer. I had to get out of the time-suck that was happening to me in El Lay. I had to escape the bullshit of the past week before I became one of the bodies left behind.

The turmoil in my mind wasn't worth the time I devoted to it. The only problem was, I had no idea where I was going next.

Although—there was this little place I heard about from an old biker when I was down Mexico way. It was out in the high desert, to the east. Maybe I'd check it out on my way through. There was something else I had to find out first. "When I leave, will you ride with me?"

I should have bit my tongue. I didn't want the question to scare Danielle off. Mostly, I didn't want to scare myself off. I waited a long time for an answer while the dishes in the sink got washed and dried and put away. Hell, this woman was an expert in procrastinating, too.

"Yes, I'd like to."

Finally. But there was another pregnant pause.

"Do I want to? I don't know. I'm settled here—or I was, until someone torched the diner."

It was obvious Danielle was agonizing over the decision. Hell, if she was smart, she'd kick me to the curb for getting her into all the shit she found herself suddenly swimming in.

"Everything that's gone on has me on edge. Meeting you. The club getting firebombed. The murder in the apartment. Even the diner last night. I don't know what to think."

"I understand. I'm the jinx that caused it all," I said. We both knew it.

"No, it's not like that. It's just—I don't know."

"Would you like some time?"

"Yes. That's what I need."

I knew what I had to do. It wasn't my style to up and leave while I owed. First on the list would be repaying Vince the five hundred. Once I did that, I'd be free and clear. He could keep my salary. I didn't need it since finding the sofa cash.

I thought I just might head east, up into the hills. I could check out that place in the high desert. It would be new ground, maybe just what I needed to take my mind off my problems of the past week. New ground sometimes held new opportunities.

Would Danielle be coming with me? I had no idea. I liked her. There was no doubt about that. As well as I knew her, she seemed to be sensible. But just like the others, I didn't know much about her or her background—other than she wasn't afraid to give me a healthy smack on the back of the head when I deserved it.

She was definitely a one-man woman. She refused to let me hustle her that first night we met in La Bonita. Considering the last two women in my life, there was something to be said about that.

I had plenty of doubt about whether I could be faithful to one woman—even one I cared for. Certainly I couldn't use the last two as a springboard. What the hell had I known about them? Whatever the outcome, I already knew I was going to give Danielle a chance if she'd let me.

I had nothing to lose.

30

I said so long to Danielle and rode like the wind to get to the club. No way could I skip out on Vince and leave him hanging for the advance I owed him. I was determined to repay him. I still didn't arrive fast enough to take the phone call Vince answered for me. I walked into the office as he was hanging up.

"That was Danielle. Jake, her ex, is beating on her door and yelling your name."

"What?"

"You heard me. Let's go."

I couldn't let him do it. It was my problem, and it was my fault. I was the one to handle it if I was ever going to have anything with the woman.

"Thanks for the offer, but you don't have any skin in this, Vince. I need to do it alone." All I needed was to get Vince involved in my mess. I figured it was bad enough I was so deep into it I could barely breathe. I'd been holding my nose for far too long.

"Are you sure?

I handed over the five hundred. He didn't even look at it.

"Do me a favor. Give Bull a call and tell him what's going on. See if he'll meet me a couple of blocks away from Danielle's at the diner."

If I could help it I didn't want to give her boyfriend a warning. The situation Danielle found herself in was my fault. Jake already beat the shit out of her once. There'd be no telling what he'd do for an encore. I had to get to her.

I raced to the burned-out diner and parked in the empty lot. I paced back and forth, waiting for Bull. I thought about going it alone until I heard squealing tires announce his arrival. The car rocked as he hurried to get out.

"How do you want to handle this?"

Bull was the expert, after all. My rescuing him from the walking fireball he became didn't hurt, either. "Who set fire to this place?"

"I'm not sure, but I think it could be related to who tossed the Molotov at the club," I said.

Bull shrugged. It wasn't his problem.

"Danielle's place is a couple of blocks away, not so far to walk. From what Vince heard on the phone, I don't know if this Jake guy is just plain nuts or regular nuts. He's been hassling Danielle since they broke up. Do you think we should call the cops?"

"No. It'll take them time to get here with a swat team, Frank. Let's go take a look," Bull said. "If he's got Danielle, he's crazy. How do you want to handle this?"

He was as worried for Danielle as I was. "We don't have a lot of time. He asked for me, so I guess I'm the guinea pig," I told Bull.

"That's all well and good, but we better scout the place before we do something stupid, don't you think?"

"You're right," I said.

We fast-trotted to the corner. Danielle's bike was parked in the driveway where it was last night.

"Give me your phone, Bull." I punched in Danielle's number. I recognized Tammi's voice when she answered. I hung up."

"That was quick."

"Tammi is in on it. There's two of them—one crazy and the other strung out on drugs," I said.

"How bad do you think it's going to be?" Bull wanted to know.

"Jake is jealous. He slashed Danielle's tires at the club and beat her up. I don't know how far he'll take it."

"What's he jealous of? How do you know where Danielle lives? Is there something you're not telling me? What the hell is going on?"

Shit. Now Bull was the one asking questions. "Can it wait until later? We have things we need to do."

"What about Tammi? What do you want to do with her?"

"At best, she's tweaking. More likely she's completely run off the rails. There's no telling what she's capable of. I think she murdered Grant, but I have no proof."

I had to get inside. I had to get Danielle out of there and away from those two crazies.

"I'm going around back to have a look. You stay in front in case someone comes out."

"No one will get by me if they've got Danielle," Bull assured me.

I believed him. I climbed onto the rear porch. I pushed at the open door. It creaked on its hinges and bumped against a chair in the empty kitchen. The jean jacket Danielle wore on our ride lay on the floor. Someone cut it in half from top to bottom. I walked through the rest of the empty house and met Bull on the front lawn.

"Nothing. Nobody home."

A drug-addled woman and a jealous, angry ex could do a lot of damage to Danielle if they thought she was responsible for their problems. Given how they'd reinforce each other's beliefs about who was to blame, I had to get her away from those two crazies as fast as I could. Unfortunately, it was going to have to wait until I located them.

"What the hell? Where could they have gone?"

"I have a pretty good idea. How would you like to meet me for a drink at El Diablo?"

"The Diablo? That dump? You think?" Bull asked.

"I know. Here's what we're going to do."

Bull made for the rear of El Diablo from the alley parking lot. I remained out front to watch for things that might want to slither out. Men in a hurry bolted through the lobby and onto the sidewalk. Behind them, the fire alarm blared through the open door. I pushed past, going in the opposite direction, and met up with Bull at the bar.

"It worked," he said. "That alarm cleared this place faster than a bomb threat."

"I hoped it would get results. Have you seen them? Are they even here?" I looked around the almost empty club. The fire alarm trick did its job. "They've got to be here. Where else could they go?"

I walked up to the darkened stage. The plastic shower stall lay in a broken pile of junk on the floor. A single overhead light shone down, illuminating a single chair.

What the hell? Was that Jake? A naked dancer, her back to the bar, leaned over a man sitting in the chair. In the shadow created by her body, the man's face was unrecognizable. The dancer's hips gyrated, forcing her crotch against his face.

Something wasn't right about that picture. It couldn't be part of a show. There was no music. Men weren't permitted on-stage during a dance. A flash of light reflected from beneath the stage light, and someone I hadn't noticed moved toward center stage.

I yelled. The woman brandished a knife. She whirled around and stumbled. The knife moved in unsteady circles. "Frank. I figured on you showing up."

The shit-eating grin pasted across Tammi's face turned into a scowl the minute she recognized me. Jake jumped off the chair and the naked dancer tumbled onto the floor. Christ. It was Danielle. What else could possibly go wrong?

The floor lights dimmed and Tammi's play-list boomed from the speakers across the room. I jumped up on the stairs and made for the pile of bodies. I had to get Danielle out of there before she got hurt. Or worse.

I was only half-way up the steps to the stage when I witnessed Danielle's foot planted square into Jake's groin. He grunted, clutched at his balls, and took a bow. He crashed down on top of her. She gave him another one between the legs for good measure and struggled on her hands and knees to crawl out from under him. He stayed down and doubled over.

Tammi didn't look happy at the condition of her new partner in crime and drug-dealing. She scowled and pointed the k-bar's steel blade at Danielle and advanced toward her. I put myself between the two of them and made a lunge for Tammi. She attempted to move out of the way, but it was no contest. She stumbled and tripped over her own feet and fell flat.

Like a turtle on its back, her arms and legs flailed. I made a grab for her wrist and twisted. She fought to keep control of the knife. She screamed in pain and released it. It fell out of her hand and clattered onto the floor. I let go and she curled up beside it.

I wasn't taking any chances. I kicked at the knife and it skidded across the stage before falling off the edge. Tammi looked up at me. Tears started and she began sobbing incoherently. She struggled, trying to breathe past the slobbering.

"Why wouldn't you listen to me? All you had to do was take me north like I wanted. None of this would have happened. You didn't listen. You never listen."

In between the sobbing and the shaking, it was hard to understand the words coming out of her mouth. "It makes no difference."

"You didn't listen. Can't we forget everything and start over?"

She actually believed that could happen. I had to set her straight. In her condition, I doubt she'd understand even simple English.

"That's not going to happen."

"Just the two of us. Please?" she continued to beg.

"Not now. Not ever. There's nothing left for us."

Danielle stood over her attackers, breathing rapidly, trying to catch her breath. Out of the corner of my eye I saw her give Jake another kick.

Where the hell had Bull gotten to? Then I saw him. The fireplug of a man had been busy holding back the bartender and a couple of the customers.

"Bull. Danielle needs your jacket," I called to him.

I had to get her out, but damned if I was going to put her out into the street naked. I didn't expect what came next.

"That won't do, Frank," she said. "It's too short. Give me your shirt."

I handed it over and she looked at me, quizzically. She knew me well enough to know there was something on my mind. She looked pretty good covered in sweat and smeared makeup. Hell, she looked good without any makeup.

"I'd do you." For my troubles, I earned an exasperated look.

"That's what's on your mind?"

"Sort of."

"If you don't get me out of here, you'll never do me again."

I took the hint and got a move on. We hooked up with Bull and made our way out of the club.

It was all over for Tammi but the crying. She had a new patsy now. Jake would probably serve her faithfully until she could find another sucker. If he was lucky and smart, he'd get away with his life. Right now, he didn't seem so smart to me, but who was I to talk?

"What are we going to do with those two? Do you want the cops to get involved?"

"I don't want anyone to get involved, Frank. I just want to get out of here and go home."

"Bull, take her out and put her on the back of my bike. Be sure she doesn't fall off when the adrenalin runs out."

It was time to lay down the law. I waited until Danielle disappeared. I didn't want her to know how I intended to solve the problem.

I arrived in time to see Jake. He was down on all fours, crawling across the stage in an attempt to get away from what he must have known would be coming. I leveled a foot against his face. He went down on his stomach, just like Grant had back in Bombay Shores.

This one wasn't smart enough to stay down. He struggled to get up on his hands and knees. I planted another boot. It finished him. He halted his struggle and stayed on his stomach, gurgling and spitting teeth out of his bloodied mouth.

He made an attempt at talking, but I wasn't planning on doing any listening. I wasn't finished with the man. For good measure, I made sure Tammi was watching. I smashed his head into the pole. I doubted she'd remember. She was stoned and out of it. Still, it felt pretty good.

Mission accomplished. Time to get the hell out before the cops showed up.

I remembered passing a door on my way into the Diablo through the lobby. I made for it and discovered the broom closet and a mop that looked like it hadn't been used in forever. I returned to the bar and collected a pack of matches and a bottle of the best high-test whiskey. I poured a generous amount of alcohol on the mop and dumped the rest on the floor. I lit a match and used it to ignite anything and everything.

I held the fire to the mop-head and waited until it caught. For good measure, I waited just a little longer before tossing everything into the closet. I made sure to leave the door slightly open. Satisfied at the orange glow peeking out, I left the El Diablo behind. No charge for the remodel.

Danielle didn't look so good sitting on the back of my bike. My shirt covered up the good parts. What wasn't covered was bruised and bloodied. Whoever did her makeup had smeared it across her face. In other words, she was one hot mess. She shook like there would be no tomorrow—but I knew different.

We both had a tomorrow.

"I thanked Bull for you and sent him home. He said to tell you if you ever need anything, to give him a call."

"Thanks." I guess Bull felt he was still in my debt, but I wouldn't be around long enough to use him ever again.

I threw a leg over and Danielle clung to me all the way to her place. I shut down in the driveway and leaned the bike over.

"Am I going to have to wipe my seat down after you slither off?"

She smacked me so hard on the back of my head I thought I'd fall off the bike. By now the adrenalin was gone, and we started to laugh. All we had left was each other. I was just happy to be here.

"Damn you, woman. Don't ever do that again."

"Only when you deserve it."

"I wasn't talking about the head-smack. I was talking about your performance on stage. Who did your makeup?"

She dropped the shirt and walked up the steps, naked. Not bad. I didn't make it a secret I was watching. When she got to the top she turned."

"Are you still packed and ready to go?

"Yes, I am."

"Give me a few minutes. I want to take a shower and make myself presentable."

"Darlin', you're never not presentable. I was in back of you watching you climb those steps."

"I knew you were watching me when I climbed the steps to the diner too, remember?"

She had me there. When Danielle came out of the bedroom, her bruises were covered with clothes. She even had a little makeup on. Very little.

"You clean up pretty good."

"I would have invited you to share the shower but I wasn't in the mood."

"That's all right. You don't have to make excuses."

"You were packed up before I was, Frank. Do you have any idea where you're headed?"

"I heard about a little place out east off the 62. It's up the hill in the high desert. I think I might hole up there for a while. What about you?"

"I don't know. I can't stay here any more. I don't want to go back to the Bonita. I can't go to the diner. It's gone, too."

"First off I'm headed out to Arizona for a few days. I'm going to pick up a houseboat from a friend and spend a few days floating on the river. You're welcome to come—no strings."

wondered what happened with the old man. He appeared to be the only sourpuss in the place.

I ate in a hurry and paid up with a healthy tip to boot. Sandy mentioned the place next door had some old bikes on display. I walked over to check them out. By then the old-timer had relocated his wrinkled fat ass and planted it in a decrepit wooden chair in the bike shop.

Something told me I needed to beat a path past the miserable excuse for a man in a hurry and get to the door. On the way I spied the help-wanted posters. One was for a clothing manager and another for something called a ride coordinator—whatever the hell that was.

At the counter I got a long-winded explanation from a name-tag that said Jack. I didn't mind so much any more. I suddenly had plenty of time. He finished and handed me an application.

I figured I didn't know anything about clothes except for what I was wearing. On the other hand, a ride coordinator sounded just about my speed.

Better yet, the job was part-time.

I filled out the paperwork and left my friend's phone number in Bluewater. If anyone thought I was qualified, they could reach me there. Then I forgot all about it.

Before I pulled out of the parking lot, I hesitated for only a moment. The road was clear. Traffic was virtually non-existent. Without another thought, I pulled onto the highway and headed east, toward the Colorado.

It was time for something new.

31

A **familiar voice called** my name over the bike shop's PA system alerting me to a phone call. I didn't get many calls. Few people knew where I worked. I picked up in the tiny upstairs office where I sometimes worked and said my usual *Hello.*

"Go back to where you came from or I'll chase you there with a forty-five."

I didn't recognize the voice. The caller didn't give me a chance to say word one before the phone went dead. If he had, he would have heard my *Go fuck yourself* response. The chair scraped as I pushed back from the desk.

My face must have turned white, because Patsy was looking at me strangely. "What's wrong?" she asked.

Before taking the time to reply, I tried a dial-back on the number. It went to a busy signal. No number came up. So much for the antiquated phone system in this miserable, dust-blown excuse for a business.

After making my way out of El Lay, I settled in the

middle of a dusty high-desert sand pit that somehow survived into the 70s. The only trouble was that it was the twenty-first century.

I tried retrieving the number a second time and still came up with nothing. I gave it up as a lost cause.

"Don't take this the wrong way, but someone just threatened my life," I said to Patsy. How the hell else could she take it?

"Are you going to call the police?" she wanted to know.

It was a question, but it came out as though that should be my next logical, common-sense step. And it would have been, but for one slight problem. I was on the run. I made my way out of El Lay's big city and bright lights in a hurry. Circumstance piled on and I narrowly escaped a murderous woman and the new boyfriend in her life.

I say new boyfriend, because I was the old she wanted dead. Well, okay, I was the old boyfriend who just happened to have pissed the woman off by having a new girlfriend.

Did I mention it was complicated?

Instead, I made an executive decision and let Patsy know I must have misheard the person on the other end of the line. She looked at me, waiting, and I promised her I had no enemies I knew about. She took me at my word and went back to concentrating on her spreadsheets in her ongoing attempt to locate missing bike-shop funds.

In the meantime, I grabbed a breath of fresh air out in the parking lot and dialed up an old biker friend on my flip phone. Snuffy was an ex-cop and ex-firefighter from Torrance. He'd been riding motorcycles all his life. Old-time biker that he was, the man had answers for everything.

I made a try at explaining as best I could. He convinced me to hang up and come up the hill for an air bath out on his patio. He'd make the tea while he waited. Damned if Snuffy was the only local I knew who offered tea. Some might have a problem with that. I didn't. Besides, I was become accustomed to it by now.

I fired up the bagger and steered her up the hill to Snuffy's. He had a main house and a smaller place in back, with a huge garage to boot. He heard me coming and had the fence unlatched. I drove through and parked. He met me in front of the house.

"It sounds to me like you've got a snoot-full of trouble, friend." Snuffy didn't like to waste words when a few would do.

"Well, considering that I don't drink with this snoot, I'd say you're right about the trouble."

"Maybe you should start." He smiled at me.

Maybe I should at that. "Hell, Snuffy, all I wanted to do was get my ass out of the city on my way to a new life. I should have known I wouldn't be able to run. I should have stayed and handled it."

"Maybe the phone call isn't related to your business in the city," he suggested. "Maybe it's more about what's going on down at the shop."

"You could be right about that. I'll have to do some thinking on it."

"Until you get it sorted out, I've got something for you." Snuffy disappeared into the main house and returned with a well-worn holster. It wasn't empty. He sat down and looked at me and grinned before handing over the package. "When's the last time you were at a range?"

"Here? Never."

He got up and headed for his van. "I'm driving. There's one just down the road."

It sounded like Snuffy knew a lot more about what was going on at the bike shop than he let on. He'd once been friends with the owner until they parted ways only recently. Still, I wanted him in the loop where I was concerned. I figured if I left anything out, he'd let me know, so I told him what I knew about what was going on.

He just looked at me like I didn't know shit from Shinola. "Sonny's been bangin' the hired help. His latest is that tall, skinny dish-water blonde bitch who does the finance and insurance. The problem is, she's taken to spying on all the employees and reporting back to the boss."

That was no surprise. I'd seen the two of them often enough with their heads together, talking shop like a couple of lovers. Sonny asked me to do some employee spying, too. I had to turn him down. Who the hell wants to be a weasel snitch? I figured my days were numbered after refusing, but he kept me on.

"I heard. Carol." Trouble was, Carol was married. To a county sheriff.

"Well, Sonny's got some fluff on the side now, and Carol knows about it," Snuffy continued. "For spite, she went out and banged one of his employees. The poor guy is only a kid. He's been telling everyone who'll listen—and some who won't—all about it."

"That's a new one on me."

Snuffy's forehead wrinkled when the grin took over his entire face. "Yeah, apparently the kid bought wine and flowers and shit to make it a real romantic deal. It sounds to me like the poor guy didn't know he could have dispensed with spending all that romance money on the woman. Someone should have told him he could of done her in the bathroom without locking the door."

"You're one cold motherfucker, Snuffy." We cackled like women gossiping on someone else's front lawn.

"Sometimes the truth hurts. I can't help that," he said. "So the kid's blabbing, and Sonny overhears him the one time he comes out of his office and doesn't go straight home, and the shit hits the fan."

Man, did it ever. It covered all of us—me the most, it seemed. I knew it first-hand from that phone call. "The rest of the outfit have about had a bellyful of Carol. With all of her spying and lies and fake goodwill she's lording the fact that she's banging the boss over the rest of us."

Snuffy only nodded. He'd heard it all before.

"It gets even crazier from there." He looked at me like that wasn't possible, so I do him one better and passed on a gem. "And then Sonny starts banging another one of his employees."

Snuffy's ears perked up. "No shit. Which one?" He sat up in his lawn chair and gave me the eye. I couldn't keep him waiting. I was too eager to tell the tale.

"Althea. The bookkeeper. At least, I think she's a bookkeeper."

Snuffy's grin turned into a look of astonishment.

"What? Her? She's the plain-looking thing, isn't she? Trailer trash dumber than a box of hammers."

I couldn't disagree. "Yeah. That one. The other dishwater blonde. The little short one with the stubby legs and no tits. He seems to like them with no tits. And he's stuck on her like trailer trash on Velveeta."

"Well I'll be damned," Snuffy exclaimed.

"One tall. One short. Just to balance things out, I guess. An equal opportunity employer. You're missing all the fun since you stopped coming in for breakfast in the morning."

It was true. I used to meet up with Snuffy at the diner first thing when it opened. We'd get all caught up and then he got smart and deserted the cause. Lately I too had to sneak off down the street to Carrows to gossip over breakfast.

Snuffy turned off the 62 onto a dirt road and the gun range showed up in the windshield. He pulled to a stop and the dust settled. I grabbed the holster off the front seat and we stopped at a table. He handed me the pistol. I flipped open the cylinder to check. It was empty. "Ruger. Five-shot. No hammer. This is nice. It looks brand-new."

I had to admit, it was compact. It didn't weigh much empty. It had a good feel to it, too. I pointed downrange and squeezed the trigger on the empty cylinder. It had a light pull. I knew by the twinkle in Snuffy's eyes that there was more.

"It'll take .38s or .357s." He reached into a pocket and pulled out a handful of .38s before handing them over.

I loaded five, closed the cylinder and double-handed the revolver. I squeezed off two, then two more. I saved one for last. "Nice." I let the last one go.

Snuffy pulled a handful of .357s out of the other pocket. It didn't take long to put them through. I noticed the bigger kick right off, thanks to the short barrel. "I'll take the pocket with the .357s. It's a stronger round."

"Close in is the best you'll do with that short barrel," Snuffy said. "It's not much for accuracy past 20-odd feet."

"That's no problem. If I have to use it, I'll be shaking so bad I won't be able to hit a wall anyway," I had to admit.

"Yeah, I hear that all right. It was the same with me."

Snuffy's only fee was the time I spent filling him in on what the hell was going on in the shop. Sometimes, I wondered too, but I didn't let on. We jaw-jacked back and forth telling lies until both of Snuffy's pockets were empty and I shot all the ammunition.

On the drive back to the house, he offered up some advice. "You're right-handed. Keep the spares in your left pocket. That way you can flip the cylinder, eject, and reload a little quicker and smoother."

I looked at him and wondered how he knew until I remembered he was an ex-cop. "Thanks. I'll do that."

"No you won't. If you need more than five, chances are you'll be running in the opposite direction faster than you can reload." He grinned across the seat at me. "If you're smart, that is."

"Smart is as smart does. I was thinking I'd throw the empty gun at whoever I was shooting at before I took off running."

That got a hoot out of Snuffy.

32

Danielle Shores was waiting at the bike shop, impatient, handing me stink-eye when I walked in. I knew better than to keep her waiting.

"Guess what. We're heading out to the river for the weekend," she announced. "I arranged the time off for both of us. I thought you might like to get away for a day or two."

We agreed no one needed to know we were a thing. We thought it for the best until we got our sea legs around the shop and learned who we could trust with our romance. If she wasn't careful, she would blow our cover. "So you just announced to everyone that you were banging me. Way to go." There was no harm in reminding her. "I thought we agreed not to."

She gave me the look reserved for when she thought I was being a jackass. "Oh for crying out loud. Get over yourself. I filled in your name on the time-off sheet. It's not difficult to fake your scrawl."

Okay, so maybe it wasn't such a big deal. I wondered if Patsy might have pulled any of the others aside and filled them in about the phone call threatening my life. She was the only other person who knew about it, outside of Danielle. The place was a gossip-maker's dream.

I brought Danielle up to speed concerning my visit to Snuffy's. She liked him, too, and considered him a friend. She needed to know I wasn't unprepared. I told her I was armed. The hammerless Ruger fit nice and tight under my belt against my stomach. The shirt I always wore untucked made it invisible.

That the woman was no dummy was one of the things I liked about her. She reached for my belt. I slapped her hand away and she touched air.

"Gun or knife?" she wanted to know.

The shirt concealed my Buck 110 as well. It was strapped to my belt and hung over the edge of my back pocket. It was in a what I called a quick-draw holster. If I needed to pull it out, it came out open and locked. There was no sense in getting caught short-handed.

"Both. And no, you can't see. No one needs to know."

Danielle turned out to be the other woman in my all-too-short El Lay adventure. She was a server at the peeler bar who volunteered an ear for my sad tale of woe. When it came to my turn, I listened to her own sad tale. That she rode her own was a plus in my book.

"Did I mention I reserved a boat with your friend in Bluewater? I hope you don't mind."

She definitely had me pegged. "You told me that already. I'm not senile. Yet. When are we leaving? That's how much I mind."

"I'm done at four," she said.

"I'll make arrangements. If we pack in a hurry we can ride across and be there just after dark."

We stopped for groceries before riding east across the flat, dusty expanse in the late-afternoon heat. At the state line we ran into dark. Even that didn't cool the hot night air until we were saying our hellos to my old friend who owned the pontoon boat on the Colorado.

We spent a few minutes catching up while Danielle emptied saddlebags and loaded groceries onto the boat. She fired up the engines and began tossing lines and sounding the horn. She flipped switches and lights came on. "This ship is sailing," she announced. "Climb aboard, sailor, or get left behind."

Danielle's grin said I shouldn't doubt it for a minute. I jumped on board as she slowly advanced the throttles and eased us away from the wharf. She'd taken to the huge boat on our last foray, and I was secretly pleased.

"Damn, woman, are you in a hurry or what?"

"We've got two days. I don't want to burn daylight."

"That's hard to do when it's already dark," I reminded her.

On the water the river was calm, the current slow. The water helped to lower the temperature from the hot and high we experienced riding across. It all came together to turn the day into a perfect night.

Using the full moon to navigate, Danielle took us into a small, shallow bay we discovered the last time we were on the water. She dropped anchor. The pontoon boat drifted on the chain and halted. She stripped and dived naked into the shallow water. I followed and mostly dog-paddled while she slowly floated by on her back, teasing me into following her.

We climbed aboard and stood arm-in-arm, overlooking the river on the upper deck. Danielle slipped away and returned wearing a thin summer dress to cover her perfect body. She handed me a pair of shorts. A full moon and a slight breeze stirred just strong enough to lift the skirt, revealing everything.

"Nice view." I had to admit it.

"You know it, mister."

"Yes, I do. And I want to know it even better. You're the best thing that's happened to me in a long time."

"There's something I have to tell you."

Oh-oh. It was never good when that phrase passed a woman's lips.

We stayed out on the upper deck, arm-in-arm, wordlessly looking out over the water reflecting the full moon. Danielle's lips brushed my cheek. She lowered her head to nuzzle my neck.

Whatever was coming, I was ready. I kept her close and waited. The words finally left her lips. There were only four of them.

"I think I'm pregnant."

The woman didn't beat around the bush. Now I knew why the sore nipples and achy hips she told me about back in El Lay sounded so familiar. I hadn't given it a second thought. Now, it was about to turn into all I could think about.

"Danielle— " I paused, knowing if I didn't, I'd put my foot in it. Or more likely, both feet. "I'm not happy about it, but it's not why you think. I'm worried about what's going on at the shop. If that asshole comes after me, I don't want you to get in the way. Or anyone else, for that matter." I halted, unsure of what to say next.

"About Florida—" she began. And then she changed her mind. "Let's talk about it tomorrow. We've got two days on the water."

"Then let's not waste them. We need to get this boat rocking."

The comforting sound of water slapping excitedly against the rock-and-rolling pontoons mimicked our raucous lovemaking. Eventually we were lulled into sweaty, exhausted sleep by that same sound, it having quieted more than a little without our fevered activity.

Morning looked like it would be a good day on the water. The sun was rising beneath blue sky and over water that was an even deeper blue. A light, cool breeze circulated throughout the huge pontoon boat.

I eased out of bed quietly and opened windows and doors to accommodate the breeze. In the tiny galley I prepared a breakfast of scrambled eggs to be accompanied by fresh fruit and juice. I left it to nudge Danielle awake. Her eyes opened and she smiled and stretched languidly beneath the sheet before throwing it off.

She sniffed the air. "Breakfast? I think I might keep you."

"You probably say that to all the boys that cook you breakfast. In the meantime, you'd better tell me what you were going to say about Florida before you lifted your skirt for me last night."

She couldn't halt the grin. "Don't let it go to either of your heads, but I lifted it for me, too."

The time away from the goings-on at the bike shop definitely relaxed Danielle. She went on about the dive school her parents owned, making the business sound popular and profitable. It was getting to be more than they could handle alone. They wanted her to come home and take over. For the first time she was seriously considering it.

"I know absolutely nothing about diving. You have eight months to teach me." There was more to it than that, but I had to start somewhere.

Obviously pleased, she smiled.

"Before you give me an answer to that, you need to know you're going to have to teach me to swim, too."

The grin didn't break. Either the woman was a good actor, or she meant it. "So that's a yes?" I couldn't believe it.

"How many ways are there to say yes?" she asked.

"Not enough, apparently. Now get back in bed," I said.

"My breakfast is getting cold." She mimed pushing me away.

"In that case, there's no sense getting up to eat, is there?" I tugged the sheet off the bed and stared at the naked woman in my bed on a pontoon boat. Before long, by mutual consent, we soon had it mimicking last night's fevered rocking.

Danielle slept in my arms, but already I was back at the shop, where someone wanted to chase me out of town with a gun. I had a pregnant girlfriend who worked with me in the bike shop. We had a shop owner's son who chased after his female employees like the serial sex predator he was.

What could go wrong?

I resolved to get my shit together as quick as I could and ride east with Danielle in tow. There was something about a dive shop on the laid-back Florida Keys that appealed to my sensibilities.

Not that a man threatening to run me out of town with a gun didn't help.

I steered the pontoon monstrosity to the dock where we tied off and packed up. We loaded the bikes together. I went inside to thank my friend for the loan of his boat. I pulled out some cash for gas and oil and offered it up. "Next time, I'll be happy to pay the full meal rental," I told him.

"I sure wouldn't say no to that."

We grinned back and forth until his head tipped in Danielle's direction. "You think she's the one?"

I didn't need to think about it. "If she wants to be."

"Then don't let this one get away."

All I could do was nod. "I'll be seeing you next time."

We rode back to the shop and the same old. While the away time might have felt like it lasted much longer, neither of us expected any change over the couple of days we were away.

Sonny's chest continued to stick out at having two women to bang. Every time he stood up he almost tipped over and fell on his face. Funny thing about Lulu, the man's wife, though. She didn't seem to mind in the slightest. Go figure.

Putting up with her husband's shenanigans wasn't kind to Lulu. Sonny's constant womanizing put the woman on countless diets. Her weight would balloon, and she'd brag about going on a diet. More than once, she would announce a three-pound loss, and that was the end of the diet.

I was privy to plenty of bike shop secrets. Perhaps it was because I could keep my mouth shut. I listened when someone had a story to tell. I never gossiped. I never told stories out of school. When I got invited to ride with the guys, I let someone else lead and I brought up the rear of the pack.

Sonny's old man, the bike shop owner, was a miserable asshole who liked bullying his employees. On a regular basis he'd pick one out and harangue the shit out of him until he found another victim he thought he might like better. The hateful old bastard was a tireless bully, which meant he was most of all a chicken-shit.

He liked to brag about his war exploits. I had a hard time believing any part of it. I figured he must have shit his pants so often he stopped wearing them, and the braggadocio was his cover.

My eyes managed to widen even more on the day I caught Carol in close quarters with a stranger. In fact, the quarters were so close it looked like he was dry-humping her. I was about to interject myself, until I saw the smile on the woman's face. Apparently, she didn't mind being dry-humped in the middle of the shop by a man who wasn't her husband. It wasn't Sonny, either. Apparently their honeymoon was over.

I changed direction, but not fast enough. Carol pointed me out to the man, and he pushed off and made time in my direction. I held my ground. I knew what was coming.

"You're still here."

It was a statement, not a question. I didn't know the man from Adam. I had my suspicions, though.

"Yes, I am," I said, still standing my ground.

I hung my shirt with a purpose, and it wasn't to show off my fat six-pack abs. I tucked it behind the handgun's grip. The man's eyes caught sight of the pistol sticking out ever so delicately over the top of my belt. He did a quick 180 and scrambled out the door so fast he was almost a blur. I followed and watched as he tore the door to his truck open, jumped in, and slammed it shut.

That truck about burned off the back tires screeching out of the parking lot in a cloud of smoking rubber. I made sure to wave the middle finger, hoping he was checking his six in the mirror as he squealed onto the main drag without stopping.

It was a nice feeling to know I could make a man disappear in a hurry. I had to wonder if the episode might come back to bite me in the ass.

33

I struggled to continue to care about my job in the bike shop. My greater concern was for Danielle and the baby we had coming. The small high desert town we were stuck in, while distant from the Salton Sea and L.A., was still too close to trouble. That was far from desirable as far as I was concerned.

I wanted to put it all in my rear-view, but for the money the job put in my pocket. Convincing Danielle to make good an escape with me might not be so easy. Her family dive shop business concerned me, too. Hell, I couldn't even swim. Added to that, I didn't know squat about diving or running a business. The dive shop thing only compounded the problem.

I kept picturing myself with a diver's weight belt strapped around my middle, good for only one thing, and that was dragging the business down. In that case, perhaps I knew more than I admitted, because it wasn't far from the truth.

Danielle didn't seem to mind. That was one more reason I put my faith in her. If she thought I'd be able to help, it was all good with me.

Perhaps sensing that I wouldn't be there long, I was the one forced to listen to the constantly complaining owners. The employees were lazy. They ripped them off. They didn't know their jobs. I listened and said nothing, but on the inside I seethed. The owners were raking in the cash while Sonny sexually harassed female employees who needed their jobs to survive.

Women talked. Any man that knows anything about women, knows that. Almost all the women around the shop knew Sonny was a sexual predator. The new ones usually found out by word of mouth. Sonny liked to use the *We like to get to know new employees* line. Once those words came out of his crooked mouth, it wasn't long before he would invite them to meet for a family dinner down the hill.

The lucky ones drove themselves with husband or boyfriend. The unlucky ones allowed Sonny to drive them. He would apologetically explain how Lulu, his wife, wasn't able to make it. That was how the excuse for a man operated with all the new ones.

The bike shop's latest service manager was young and tall and married. Her husband worked a lot of hours at his job, and was hardly ever home. The young woman made no bones about letting me know that Sonny had been inviting her out for a company dinner. She explained how she made it plain to the man that her husband wouldn't be able to accompany her.

That didn't stop Sonny. Prick that he was, he refused to take no for an answer. He went into full predator mode, becoming even more aggressive and insistent. Eventually, against better judgment, the woman ended up going along with him. A week later she started showing up at work dressing a little better and wearing makeup. It was a complete makeover for her.

Pity the woman who made the mistake of not bringing her husband, or boyfriend, or of not going in her own car. If she accepted Sonny's ride, it was definitely her turn in the batter's box.

Married or single, they were all the same to Sonny. He didn't pick sides. If the woman refused his advances, or even if she didn't, eventually she'd be laid off. He gave this dirty work to Fred, the general manager.

How Sonny got away without his ass being sued off, I never discovered.

Another of Sonny's favored tactics was to pay for performance. Carol ended up getting an annual ten grand bonus for her enthusiastic efforts on behalf of Sonny. The losers like Althea, who couldn't count to ten without taking a shoe off, would get five thousand. More often, his conquests ended up with nothing but their hourly rate until they were shown the door.

Of course, I didn't know any of this first-hand. I only learned about it from some of the women who took me into their confidence. I didn't consider it a kindness that they let me in on what was going on. Still, my advice was to skip the dinner entirely. Some did. Most didn't. They must have thought a free meal on the boss was a good thing. It all got me thinking that Danielle's turn with Sonny would come up soon enough.

We never made it plain or obvious that Danielle and I were a thing. We liked it that way. No one asked us silly questions. We played at being friendly, so the gossip probably made the rounds, but we kept our hands off of one another in the shop.

Even though we talked around Sonny's penchant for his female employees, we never discussed what she, or I, would do should he hit on her. In the end, we decided to leave it up to Sonny to set the agenda.

The guys at the shop did a boy's night out occasionally. I hassled them about having to get the okay from their wives or girlfriends. We'd drink beer and play snooker and smoke and tell lies about women we knew, and come up with more lies about some we didn't or would like to.

On one of these nights Danielle's name came up. I kept my mouth shut, gritted my teeth, and listened. Nobody glanced my way. Some of the comments were about her on-the-job abilities. A lot were about her good looks. I went along and agreed, but I kept it to myself that she looked even better beneath the sheets.

I bummed smokes and had a couple of beers and shot a few games, but most of these nights turned out to be pretty tame. Come 9 p.m., most of the guys made excuses and split for home and waiting wives or girlfriends. Only the die-hard partiers remained behind. I did, too, just because I wanted to.

Come midnight, I asked the bartender to call a cab. I went outside to escape the cigarette smoke and the loud music. Maybe waiting in the alley beside the bar was a mistake, but I didn't think so at the time.

The darkness concealed the men too well. They came out of the night and were on me in an instant. Unrecognizable as they were, it didn't take much to recognize the glint of sharp steel reflected off the knife. It was aimed at my stomach. It would do serious damage if it connected.

I stumbled back, and number two grabbed my arms and hung on. I rolled to the side. The motion took him with me. I ducked. The knife missed my mid-section and glanced off a rib.

The feeble attempt at a follow-through was a tough go with my arms pinned. I managed a kick at the knife hand as it went by. There was no time for congratulations when I connected. I turned again and raised both arms in an attempt to slip out of the second man's grip. An elbow doubled him over and I knew when to retreat. Lights flashed when the cab turned into the alley and I ran like hell and dived into the back seat through the open door.

I pressed a hand against my side and held on. I managed a quick look beneath my hand, but there was too much blood. I could only hope the blade didn't get a chance to dig in and do serious damage. Danielle wasn't going to be happy at the prospect of having to worry even more about my situation with the guy who threatened to run me out of town.

It had to be him. More likely, it had to be some of his friends, trying to run me off. I figured since I let him see the handgun tucked away in my belt he stayed out of it and let someone else do the talking. Or, in this case, the stabbing.

I didn't think I'd end up wrong about that. I was pretty sure Danielle wouldn't want to stay around much past payday when she finished bandaging my side. And I was doubly certain I'd be getting some words for being so stupid as to get stuck like a turkey in a back alley.

I wasn't wrong. Danielle took one look at my bleeding rib cage and ordered me onto the kitchen table. She waved scissors in my direction and cut off my bloodied shirt. She hauled out a battered first aid kit from somewhere and proceeded to wrap me in bandages. She hummed while she did it, too. I wasn't quite sure how to take that. On the other hand, I was just happy to be there.

"Well, we were right."

Oh-oh. "We were? About what?"

"Sonny called while you were out getting stabbed."

I was forced to remind her it was a night out with the boys. I didn't set out intending to allow a good stabbing to enter into it. "Carol must have overheard the guys talking about going to the bar. She knew I always tagged along." No way in hell did I think Sonny was responsible for whoever was trying to stick me with cold steel.

"No, not that. The other."

Sonny's phone call. Of course. "Do I have to ask what he wanted?"

"Nope. We got it right," she assured me.

Sure, we'd discussed it. What we hadn't talked about was what Danielle would do when Sonny made his pass. "Are you going to play along?" Like I needed to ask the question.

"That I am. And I'm going with a recorder."

Already I knew trying to talk Danielle out of it was out of the question. I hadn't known the woman for long, but I knew her enough that once she made up her mind, she didn't change it, right or wrong. That she was more than a little stubborn came to mind, but I didn't need to say it.

"Tell me what the pervert said."

I had to give her credit for knowing how to look after herself. Even so, Sonny, the experienced predator he was, probably had more than a few tricks in his bag.

"It was the usual dinner with the wife to get to know you spiel. According to word around the shop, that's the line he uses. We know how that goes down."

We did, and it ended with Sonny explaining that his wife couldn't make it because of something going on with their kids. Lies, all of it, but it worked for Sonny. "Maybe she acts as his enabler. Are you sure you want to go through with this? Can we at least talk about it before you do something you might regret?" I had to say it, even though I knew it was a done deal with her.

"My mind is made up. When I'm finished with that asshole, he's going to pay out or go down. And I don't mean down on me."

I liked hearing the pay or go down part. But I didn't like that Danielle would be subjecting herself to Sonny's advances. I didn't want to dwell on the danger. I wanted to know what she was going to use for a wire. I wanted to know what she'd do when she went with him down the hill.

"I've got most of it figured out," she tried reassuring me.

Most of it? I wanted to hold up a hand to stop her in her tracks. I didn't.

"I even know what I'm going to wear when the time comes. The only thing I haven't decided on is if you'll be there in case I need help. Extricating myself from the mess that's going to go down in the parking lot of that shitty steak house might be more than I bargained for."

Those were words I wanted to hear. The place he

took all of his victims was once a renowned eatery. At one time, it was the place to go, but its red velvet interior was tired and dated. Second rate. Old people ate there. How modern could that make it?

Danielle knew I'd back her up if she needed it. In fact, I'd already rescued her once when I pulled her naked ass out of the seedy El Diablo strip club. I had no compunction about doing it again. "When you make up your mind how it's going to go down, I'll be all ears."

But would she tell me? I had my doubts. Did I mention the woman was stubborn?

"The only thing left to decide is which one of my tits that asshole is going to get to see."

Now I knew she was serious. I didn't get to see either of them for a couple of days after we first met. She caught me grinning.

"I know what you're thinking. I knew you were trouble the instant I saw you checking me out in the club."

I couldn't disagree with that.

34

My **biggest problem turned** out to be convincing Danielle to ride to the scene of the crime. I wanted her to scope out the restaurant's parking lot for a spot that would serve her purpose. She refused to take me seriously. "It's for your own safety," I insisted. "You don't want to be out there without a plan. If you must know, I'm the one that doesn't want you out there with no plan."

"You're overthinking it."

But I wasn't, and she'd never convince me otherwise. "Do you want to be riding aimlessly around the lot looking for a place to park? Or would you rather drive into the lot and go right to where you want to be?" I paused to give her a chance to think about it. "What if the best spot is occupied? What's the alternative? What's your third choice?"

She rolled her eyes like we were back in high school. Come to think of it, that's pretty much how the dealership operated, with its tattletale employee and the owner's son trying to screw the female help like he was a former high school football hero. Funny thing about that, though. He was a former teacher. In a moment of weakness, Lulu told me he hated the job so much he quit and went to work in a butcher shop. Given Sonny's proclivities for his female employees, I wasn't surprised in the slightest, and wondered what the real reason was.

"You're not going to ride down the hill in a dress. Where are you going to change? If Sonny shows up just as you pull into the lot, do you want to be riding around looking for a parking spot where you can do the deed? Or would you rather have him follow you to plan A?"

Danielle didn't respond right away. I wanted to grab her and give her a shake.

"All right. Jeez. We'll go."

"It's all about situational control. You want as much control over what happens as you can get. You won't regret it." I shut up before she changed her mind.

The plan was to ride down the hill to the restaurant's parking lot and have a look see. We were looking for an area that was dark and inviting enough that Sonny would follow her. We arrived to discover the restaurant's parking lot to be much bigger than we imagined. It was wide open, broken up only by trees and shrubs.

We parked and walked the lot separately, finally meeting up at a location surrounded by fence and tall, thick bushes on two sides. It looked to be ideal. The site backed onto a fenced motel lot. The fence would do double duty by blocking the view and keeping it shadowed from the motel's night lighting.

"You can't hide it, can you?" I was grinning at her.

"Nope. Great minds think alike. That corner is the one. We can leave now."

We had our location worked out. I wanted to scout out the interior. "Are you sure? Maybe we should check out the restaurant."

Danielle shook her head almost too fast. Her hair cascaded over her shoulders. Not a chance. I don't want anyone recognizing me. Hearing *Back again so soon?* might give Sonny a clue. That'll surely put a crimp in the deal."

She convinced me. We saddled up and pulled out onto Piñon, headed north. I worried how Danielle would handle Sonny. He wasn't a big man, but he was taller than she was, and stronger, too. She'd handled Jake on the dance floor of the El Diablo, but this was turning into something else. He would have her in the close confines of his truck.

I had to get her talking about how she planned to handle the man. If she even had a plan. The way this was coming together was starting to make me more than a bit uncomfortable.

I waved to her and she rode on ahead before we got to Buena Vista. There was no sense alerting the troops we might be hanging out after-hours. The gossip mongers would have a field day with that bit of intel.

Just before the crest of the hill a blip and flashing blues forced me to the side of the road. I shut down and stayed on the bike, just like every other biker before me. I left my hands in plain sight on the handlebars. I didn't want to be seen as tempting fate.

The usual inanities came out of the cop's mouth. I

handed over the papers and sat back to wait. When he returned, I almost did a double take when I spied the name tag on his uniform shirt.

"I heard you're the guy that got the threatening phone call."

That was news to me, considering I had never reported it. In fact, I never reported anything to a cop, ever. "I wouldn't know anything about that. Am I free to go?" The standard question when it appeared as though the traffic stop was over.

He handed back my papers and I left for the bike shop. Something was going on that I wasn't a party to. By now I figured I knew who the loudmouth was, and how this guy got the story.

Hell, maybe he was the story.

At the diner I took a seat beside the pie rack. It was my regular place at the counter. Sandy was on duty, a short, sweet little thing with red hair, a ready smile, and a hearty laugh. We got along well in the small restaurant. She liked to gossip and I liked to listen. Sandy was my go-to. I used her to get caught up on the trials and tribulations of the bike shop's employees.

She gave me a warm greeting, and I knew something was coming up. Before long, she was taking delight in telling me how she'd divorced her old man. In the process, she explained she ended up the proud possessor of most of the man's construction equipment as part of the settlement. Every time she needed a little extra cash, she'd sell another piece of equipment and grin on the way to the bank.

I wanted to ask what her old man did that she ended

up with everything. Instead, I gave her a high five. I figured she'd tell me when she wanted to.

The diner was done in a 50s style, with a counter and stools fronting the open grill. Booths lined the opposite wall. An entrance to a patio with tables split the booths in half. The diner wasn't huge, but the place was popular and a destination in itself with the biker crowd. Locals too came to enjoy the good food.

The cooks were what made the place, of course. But for the one woman slipping cash from the till into her pocket, there was a steady stream of them, and they all were pretty competent. The servers did for the rest with a steady stream of banter, both for the regulars and those stopping in from out of town.

The one thing that made the diner uncomfortable was Pappy, the hate-filled, senile old owner of the place. The miserable excuse for a man would come in first thing in the morning at 7 a.m. when the diner opened.

He'd take up a regular spot in his booth and scream at Sandy for spending too long with the customers, or not long enough. She laughed too loud. She walked too slow. The hate-filled old bastard could never keep his story straight. It was one of the many things that made him the laughingstock of the business.

It got so bad, even the local police stopped showing up for lunch. It occurred to me that the captain might have gotten some complaints about Sonny's sexual proclivities concerning the women in the shop. It wouldn't surprise me that more than one might have complained.

Pappy liked regaling anyone who would listen with the story of how he had retired in the high desert to open a bike shop. He needed something to do, he said.

He took his business to a local bank. Before long, Annabelle, a teller, caught the fish out of water. She had the hateful old man reeled in hook, line, and sinker before she left the bank for greener pastures as Pappy's wife.

Annabelle took over the day-to-day running of the bike shop by hiring up a bunch of people sympathetic to her plight. Given how useless the old man was, I couldn't blame her. By the time I arrived, the place was being run into the ground, and the greener pastures didn't last long. Employee theft, cash loans to employees who were liars and cheats were all doing their damnedest to push the business over the edge.

Pappy finally got smart, something he wasn't known for, and brought in his son. Sonny took over the day-to-day running of the business as it teetered on the edge of bankruptcy.

Before long, Annabelle, the wife, was gone. Sonny was banging Carol. The old man kept up his crazy, simple-minded tirades against any employee that would listen to him. Unfortunately, there were more than a few that needed the job and the steady income to feed their families, and thus were forced to put up with it.

Eventually, Sonny came to see the place as a smorgasbord of willing female employees he could take advantage of. I'm sure Carol saw the same once she ran her hand up his thigh and discovered the size of his pencil dick. She tried that with me shortly after I discovered the place. I was glad now I'd taken her hand away and placed it on her own thigh. To keep the peace, I gave her a squeeze and told her not now. Like that would ever happen. As long as she thought it might was all right with me.

No Way Out

Perhaps the saddest part of it, or the most terrifying, depending on one's position, was that Carol's husband was the cop that pulled me over. Surely he couldn't be the one that made the phone call.

Or could he?

35

It was quitting time for me. I pulled out of the parking lot and nicked into second. I twisted the throttle and was well on my way to third. In the rearview I caught a black half-ton going around me in the outside lane. I couldn't say I was unprepared.

The truck's turn signal was showing a left turn, an impossibility in the traffic bearing down in the opposite direction. The driver pulled in front of me, as I suspected. I covered the front brake like I was in El Lay traffic. I used the rear and reduced throttle to help bleed off speed.

The truck's brake lights flashed and instantly went solid, like the driver changed his mind. At almost the same instant, I grabbed a handful of front and stomped on the rear.

Motorcycles are lighter than every other vehicle. They tend to stop quicker when both brakes are applied and the tires don't lock up. Locking up tires on a big, heavy bagger was not easy. The last time it happened, I was on a fresh-painted traffic line when I was forced to brake. My front wheel locked and skidded briefly until I could lighten my grip.

Not so this time. Dry pavement and judicious application of practiced panic braking maneuvers saved my ass. Well, okay, that, luck, and horseshoes weighing me down would be my guess as to why I missed out on the road rash.

The hothead in front of me jumped out of the truck without closing the door. Before I could get the kickstand down, he was on me with a flying tackle. My ride tipped and I rolled off and pulled up my leg before it fell onto its side. So much for the new paint.

I barely avoided the weight of the falling bike. I rolled upright, unsteady on my feet. The dumbass was in a hurry to beat the shit out of me. I dropped. He wasn't expecting that. I kicked with a sweeping right boot. I connected with his knee. He collapsed on the ground with a scream and a thud.

I laid a second boot to him. It sunk into his beer belly. That one kept him on the ground for sure, right beside my ride. When I had time to look, I discovered it was the man I ran out of the shop. Giving him a peek at the handgun tucked into my belt did the deed then.

It wasn't long before the black and white arrived. I ended up patted down and handcuffed before being loaded into the back. With nothing else to do, I kept an eye on officer friendly, who was in deep conversation with my assailant. He wasn't about taking my statement. He had to have been watching it all go down to arrive on-scene so fast. More than likely the two were in cahoots.

When the flatbed arrived, it sounded like double

jeopardy when I heard the cop tell the driver to haul it up on its side. He did, and I knew for sure what transpired. I was in deep shit, and all I ever did was piss off a cop's wife I happened to work with. Sometimes, life wasn't fair that way.

And sometimes, what goes around comes around to bite you in the ass.

There were no wants or warrants out on me, but then, the cop already knew that. He was the same one that pulled me over earlier in the day while I was returning from the scouting mission down the hill. The bastard wouldn't take an accident report, either. He said there had been no accident.

Which, technically, I suppose, was true.

Officer friendly cast a smug look in my direction as he climbed into the driver's seat. I casually mentioned the video someone was making. It was being filmed by one of the women at the bike shop. I didn't tell him her name.

From the back seat, I looked out the window at the woman and nodded. She waved and pointed skyward. By the look of it, the video was already in the cloud.

I didn't wait for a reaction from the cop. I could afford to be cocky. Snuffy's handgun was at home, safely tucked beneath the bed and not in my waistband.

Hours later, I walked out of the cop shop, free and happy. The way things were going, I figured the cops would be next in line to tell me to hit the high road for my own good. Since Carol's old man was familiar with my circumstances, I pretty much knew she was the one to tell her cop husband about the phone call at the shop.

Smartass that I was, I wondered if she ever took the time to tell him he had been cuckolded by Sonny. It was the old guilt by association thing. Being a cop, he could associate a lot of guilt by means of his wife's lover, Sonny, and anyone who worked for him in the bike shop.

My freedom didn't last long. A couple of deputies took it upon themselves to accost me again. I was hauled back to the station. They double-timed me into a cell and slammed the door. I waited patiently to hear the charges to go along with the incarceration.

In the meantime, it was desert-hot outside, and air-conditioned on the inside. I made good use of the break while I waited.

I didn't get to make a phone call. No one showed up. The smell I detected wasn't coming from my feet. Something wasn't right, and it wasn't me. I settled in for a long wait. I checked the mattress for bed bugs and stretched out when I didn't find any.

Someone must have taken exception to my snoring. Every couple of hours a guard would rattle the bars to keep me awake. Until the door opened, I figured there wouldn't be much to be concerned about.

Except for one thing.

Danielle had an invitation to meet with her boss for dinner. Our plan had been for me to wait things out in the parking lot in case things went sideways and he went for a full-blown assault and rape right there.

I knew for a fact sexual assault was already a huge part of Sonny's menu. I wondered if getting thrown into a jail cell for absolutely no reason was part of the same menu.

With nothing but time on my hands, I went through all the ways I knew to hurt a man.

36

Three bills later, I was released for the second time. It cost me that much again to get my ride out of impound. I didn't have any complaints, though. Run-ins with cops were all part of the deal. It was the biker way. I got the message, too. Don't make waves. Don't make waves about anything. With one exception, I was in full and complete agreement.

I made it home in time to meet Danielle. Already she was on her way out the door and headed for work.

"I got called in to work the Friday evening shift," she explained. "I heard you ended up in jail."

The high desert wind had no doubt been blowing through town, spreading rumors along with the sand and dust. This time, it was no rumor.

"Yes I did. Carol's cop-husband pulled me over just after you pulled away. He ended up hauling me off to county after I clocked out of the bike shop."

"What did he charge you with?"

"Nothing. I'm typical biker trash, apparently. When I waltzed out of the building, two apes caught up with me and hauled me back. I spent the night in lock-up."

Danielle was giving me a look I didn't recognize. It was somewhere between shit-eating grin and cat-eating canary.

"What's up with you?"

"I have to get to work. I'll tell you all about it later."

She headed out the door, and I headed for the shower. I left for work a day and twenty minutes late. I never got the chance to let the boss know I wouldn't be in. I wondered if I would have a job waiting for me.

Danielle was looking pretty good in her tight jeans. She was braless under the thin top, too. Carol wouldn't be happy with that shoved in Sonny's face all day. I knew right away I'd missed all the good stuff at the restaurant down the hill.

"You had a date night, didn't you?" I asked.

She made sure to look around the shop before breaking out into a huge grin. "I did."

I sure as hell wasn't looking forward to hearing about it. I swallowed my pride and hoped I was hiding it. "And?" I figured I already knew the answer.

"It went down just as we knew it would. Can you listen without flying off the handle?"

While I hadn't been so enthused about Danielle's plan, I wasn't able to talk her out of it. At best I convinced her to ride down to the place and look it over before Sonny showed up, and we did that together.

"Considering the time we invested in talking about just such a thing, I'm pretty sure I can."

Just when the story was about to get started, Sonny

poked his head out of his office and waved me in. If I didn't know better, I'd say he didn't want me associating with Danielle.

"You spent the night in jail."

He didn't look so surprised to me.

"Word travels fast in these parts, doesn't it?"

I suspected Carol had been the one to fill him in. Her old man wouldn't have missed an opportunity to tell his wife he hassled one of her boyfriend's employees.

"I have to let you go. You didn't show yesterday, and you didn't call. I'm running a business. I can't rely on people who don't show up for work."

It came as no surprise. On the other hand, from what I knew, it was usually the other way around. Sonny's female employees were the ones that ended up getting fired. This time, the man had to be working on something else.

Although, if it was Danielle he was working on, he wouldn't want me around to witness it if he suspected we were becoming a couple. Maybe he had some inside information.

I didn't get a chance to talk to Danielle about what happened during her dinner with Sonny. Through no fault of my own, I'd been twiddling my thumbs in jail. She confirmed my suspicions, though.

"We'll meet for lunch at the usual place," she told me. "I can't wait to tell you about it."

I let her know I was fired and walked out of the bike shop for the last time. I knew I wouldn't be so eager to hear what Sonny tried to do to her, but I'd listen to what she had to say.

At the apartment I took a better look at my ride. The bike wasn't in as poor shape as I thought. Most of the damage was cosmetic and wouldn't be expensive to repair. A wash and a little wax would help. The downtime would give me an opportunity to think.

I had my suspicions about why I was fired. The way the police were treating me, it began to look like I was on the verge of being run out of town. The only thing missing was the rail I was supposed to ride.

Beginning with the phone call by someone wanting to chase me out of town with a handgun, and ending with the overnight stay courtesy of the county, I ended up without a job. It didn't take a rocket scientist to figure it out. If I knew what was good for me, I'd be getting out of town as fast as I could.

And I would, but for one thing. There was no way I was leaving Danielle on her own in the viper's nest of liars, cheats, lawbreakers and sexual predators. Even she had to know that.

I never made it to our lunch meetup. I never made it out of our apartment. The door crashed open and I found myself stuffed into the back of another black and white. The smirk on the face of officer dumbass couldn't be erased. The cursory search came up with Snuffy's Ruger. Unfortunately for me, I hadn't stashed it in the right place.

I spent another night with miscellaneous drunks and impaired drivers. This time, I got to make a phone call. I came up with a woman lawyer who, when I described my earlier incarceration without cause, marched down and negotiated me out with nary a charge. Apparently, there was a matter of a search warrant with faulty information on it

I thanked the woman profusely and convinced her to drive me back to my place. I gave her two grand from the stash I rescued from the sofa in the El Lay apartment.

The woman never batted an eye. She put the money in her purse without counting it. She advised me to get out of town as fast as I could. I thanked her and watched her drive away in her Cadillac.

I wanted to take her advice. I really did.

37

I was fast turning into one more local loser, like the guy with a stolen and repainted step-van rental truck hidden away on his desert acreage. It had only been discovered seven years after the fact when his place was raided. Given the number of meth labs lurking in the surrounding county, I couldn't figure why the local sheriff was interested in my comings and goings. For reasons unknown, I had become a thorn in someone's side.

It was that, or Sonny had an in. I couldn't get a handle on that, considering he was doing the wife of an officer. I rode up to Snuffy's to let him know the cops had his handgun.

"I'll be happy to replace it or pay for it," I told him.

He laughed. "Welcome to Buena Vista. It wasn't registered."

At least I was ahead on that one. He led me to the patio where we sat down to take another air bath. The wind rushed up the hillside, rustling leaves in the bushes surrounding his patio.

"It's been nice to know you, Frank. Now get out of town." He wasn't smiling this time.

"Damn, Snuffy, you're sounding like the locals."

"I heard your girlfriend stuck Sonny up in a parking lot."

"Danielle? Man, I haven't had a chance to talk to her about it. I keep getting put in the slammer."

"The both of you should get out as fast as you can. And out of the state even faster."

"She's got her lunch hour coming up. I think I'll ride home and pack us up." I stuck out my hand and Snuffy took it.

"You probably shouldn't come back."

"Don't worry, I never do. So long, old friend. Will you call Danielle for me?"

Twenty minutes to get home. Another ten to load the bagger as fast as I could with clothes. I was ready to hit the road. All I needed was Danielle. It would worry the hell out of me until she showed up.

I closed the trunk just as noisy pipes announced her arrival. She saw me waiting, waved and burned a U-turn. She halted and tilted her head in the direction the sun rose.

That was all I needed.

I punched the button and we were off. We rolled side-by side through intersections and corners. We hit the 62, and we were gone. We stopped at Vidal to fill the Sporty's tank. Outside of the Earp post office we waved goodbye to California, turned right and crossed the Colorado. We stopped at a gas bar for fuel.

"We're home-free, baby. Now, are you going to tell me what went down in the parking lot?"

"Snuffy called me to let me know you were

heading out."

"Yeah, I asked him to. Do I have to get back to him about what happened with you and your pal?" I asked.

"He knows about it? What the fuck." It wasn't a question.

"The desert wind doesn't only blow sand," I said.

"Apparently not. I'll be more comfortable if we had a few more miles between here and there."

Whatever happened on her date with Sonny, it had her spooked. There'd be no telling when she'd clue me in. "Saddle up. We'll take the 72 to the dogleg and the 10 and we're gone, baby. We'll be in Texas tonight.

Danielle fired up the Sporty and took off. She didn't look back to see if I was following. Before long we were on the 10 and making speed. Interstates were good for one thing, and one thing only.

We made good time. It was hot and dry into Phoenix and Tucson. The wind across the interstate was strong enough to make for some difficult riding in the sand-laden wind. We wrestled the steering and argued with the gusts as they tried time and again to force us off the asphalt.

We did the gas-and-go routine all the way across Arizona and into New Mexico. I did the fueling while Danielle went to get burritos or chicken, or whatever looked edible. Plenty of water to wash it all down ended up in saddlebags.

Bathroom breaks occurred at the side of the road, with the bikes running. I stood comfortably while

know what to think. "Where's the other half of the party?"

An open-mouthed Ava planted herself at the end of the counter with a look that said she needed to know what was going on before she gave up and ran away.

"Danielle is across the street with her folks. I left to check out the diner. I guess I can leave now, since I know how the food is going to be."

The grin halted as Eddy gave me a dirty look. "Is that a backhanded compliment?" He waved the knife again, and tilted his head in Ava's direction.

"No, it's the truth. It looks like the insurance paid out pretty good for you to pick up this place."

"Yeah, well, it needed some renos. I'm just shy of twenty in with the bank. She's a good old diner, though. I wouldn't have bought it otherwise."

"The dive shop across the street—" I didn't get a chance to finish before Eddy interrupted.

"They're good people. The day I had the key in the lock to open and they came across with fresh coffee and breakfast. They told me I shouldn't be cooking for myself on my very first day."

The cowbell rang and the door slammed. Danielle just about tripped in her haste to get to us. She cracked the back of my head. I almost fell off the stool. Eddy laughed. "I see you haven't lost your touch, lady."

My eyes watered so bad I couldn't see a thing. Through the tears it looked like Ava was getting ready to leave as fast as she could.

"Jesus, woman, don't ever do that again or I'll put you over my knee right here."

"If you'd have told me Eddy was already here, your head wouldn't be so sore."

"Sore, hell. I figured you were across the street making yourself pretty." I winked at Eddy.

"Any way I look I'm more than pretty enough for you. And don't you forget it for as long as we're together."

I ignored her, as much as I didn't want to. Ava was grinning and it looked like she wanted to stay for the fireworks now.

"Yeah, yeah, speaking of sore heads, what did you do about Sonny? You've been holding out on me for three thousand miles." It was a question I wanted answers for a lot sooner than today.

"Well, since all the important people in my life are here—" Danielle saw Ava and introduced herself.

I couldn't resist the interruption. "Eddy, you better put on a fresh pot of coffee for this. I kept my mouth shut for the entire cross-country ride, but when it's time, it's time."

38

Danielle was finally ready to tell her tale. She had all of us, including Ava, stuffed into a booth. Her audience was all ears.

"Where to start, Eddy. Where to start. Let's see—" She paused for effect, looking across at me.

"Don't rush it on my account, woman." It had been killing me on the ride all the way across, but I never let on.

"While biker boy here was slackin' it in a jail cell in the wind-blown and dusty high desert plain, I was out cruising a parking lot waiting for my boss to show up. He wasn't hard to spot once he saw the white blouse and the short skirt waving at him in the breeze.

Eddy looked at me like I was nuts to let her do it. I

only shrugged and he nodded. He knew her at least as well as I did.

"This is a first for me, too, Eddy. She never breathed a word of it the whole time."

"That's because I was afraid you couldn't take it. Now that Eddy's here, you're going to have to man up." She winked at Eddy.

Damn if this woman wasn't a piece of work. I didn't know whether to laugh or ride off as quick as I could. She seemed to know it, too. "If you do, don't bother coming back."

I eyed Eddy and he eyed me and we both knew I was whipped. He sat back and grinned and shook his head. I sat back and waited. Ava's elbows were on the table and her chin was in her hands. She was anxious for Danielle to go on.

"Earlier, Frank convinced me to ride down to the scene of the crime and scout out the parking lot looking for a good place to do the deed. While Sonny busied himself backing into the exact parking spot we picked, I managed to get a couple of buttons undone."

She looked at us, pleased as punch.

"I squeezed my nipples as hard as I could and sidled up to the door. The window went down. I leaned in like a car-hop on roller blades serving up a milkshake, and grabbed his crotch."

Ava gasped. I harrumphed. Eddy looked like he couldn't believe what he was hearing.

"Damn, woman. You knew what a mess that man was. He could have hurt you."

"Yeah. No. He tried to get the door open, but I wasn't that stupid. I had my hip braced against it. He flailed with his arm out the window and then changed his mind and put the seat all the way back. He ended up staring at the tits falling out of my blouse.

My jaw dropped just in time for Danielle to carry on. Ava looked like she wanted to be somewhere else. Eddy only nodded. He refused to look in my direction this time.

"In an instant and before he knew it, I had his pencil dick out catching wind and a breath of fresh night air."

"Eddy, where's the key to the bathroom? I don't need to hear this." I pretended to get up.

"Yes, you do, Frank."

Danielle was right. I couldn't say no now.

"I gave the pencil dick half-a-dozen strokes and felt him getting harder. I squeezed the son of a bitch off just to coat his balls with blue and started swinging my hips in the direction of the restaurant. Damned if I was going to miss out on a free meal.

She had a satisfied look on her face, but her story wasn't finished. Neither was Sonny by the sound of it. I looked over at Ava. Her mouth hadn't changed its expression. It was still open.

"I sidled up to him in the booth and had my hand everywhere but his crotch. By the time I finished with him, the man was so horny I thought he was going to stroke out on me right there in the booth, and I don't mean by stroking his own dick."

Danielle was on a roll, no doubt about it. Eddy and I were trying to avoid looking at one another. I don't think either one of us wanted to believe her, but we weren't sure. Danielle caught her breath and went on while looking across at Ava.

"When the check came, Sonny handed me the keys.

I hurried out to the truck and waited. When he got in I spread my legs and flashed more tit. Before I could say a word he had his dick out. I bent over and went for it like I was going to suck the life out of him."

Here we go.

"Don't panic, boys. I gave him a handy. When he finished blowing his load, I told him if he wanted something else that was warm, wet and welcoming to slip into, it would cost him double the bonus he was handing over to Carol."

She halted briefly and looked across at all three of us, one at a time. "Cash in advance."

I couldn't believe what I was hearing. Now I knew the reason she was glued to her sporty and the saddlebags all the way across.

"The next day, the fool paid up, I tucked it away, rode out of town before he changed his mind, and here we are."

"You just told me more than I wanted to hear, girl."

"Yes, well, now it's your turn. Is there anything I need to know about you?"

I looked at Eddy once more, and he did more head shaking. "You better do as she says, Frank. If you don't stick with this one, I'll hunt you down myself."

"I think you're right. She's worth every nickel—or every thousand, at least."

That was Danielle's sign to get up and walk out of the diner. She wasn't gone all that long before the cowbell over the door rang again. She approached the counter in front of Eddy and dropped what must have been close to twenty large on the counter.

"Pay it off, Eddy. You need to own it in full. And yeah, mom told me all about it."

The man didn't know what to do. He stood back and looked toward the door. He checked the windows. He crossed his arms and looked up at the ceiling as though invoking a higher power before looking over at Ava. She managed to close her mouth, at least.

"Ava. How much do you owe on that beater you bought?"

The dark-haired, older version of Danielle who told me to sit anywhere stood up and moved behind the counter beside Eddy.

"A little over nine hundred and change," she admitted. "Why? And it's not a beater. It's been pretty reliable for me."

Eddy counted out a thousand and handed it to the woman. "I just came into some money, and I like to share with friends and neighbors. There's a little extra for gas."

Fortunately, the woman already had a hand on the counter to steady herself. "Oh, Eddy. That's not right. You can't."

He fished beneath the counter and came up with an envelope. He slipped the thousand into it before putting it back under the counter. "You know where it is when you need it."

The cash was no loss to either of us. We believed we had it coming, considering what we went through. Hell, Dani had earned hers. I knew what was left of mine to be a gift I stumbled across for enduring two women and their companions who wanted to see me dead.

I was pretty sure Dani had wormed her fee out of Sonny for the promise that he'd make her another notch when he forced her over his office desk.

"Eddy, if you've got questions, you're going to have to save them for later. I've got eight months to teach this one how to swim before he becomes a permanent baby-sitter."

Danielle grabbed my ear and yanked me off the stool. I cast a sidelong glance in Eddy's direction, but his eyes were closed and his hands covered his ears. I called across to him.

"I need some help here, man."

Eddie's eyes opened and went wide.

"I'm not a man known to be giving advice, but just to be safe, I'd say learn to dog paddle first."

More Frank Ross Road Trips

Midnight at the Oasis
Bank Robber Dames
Fast Food Slow Waitress
Bad Girls

Print Books by P X DUKE

Jim Nash The Beginning
Gun Crazy
Gun Crazy 2
Gun Crazy 3
Fallen Angels
Last Stop to Nowhere
Revenge Is Justice
Escape / Forget Me Not
Wedding Bell Blues / Breakdown
Mexico Time
No Free Ride / Gone

Dead Reckoning
Uncharted
Go-Around

No Way Out
Bank Robber Dames

The Last President

SIREN ON THE RANGE

RED HART RANCH
BOOK 2

SOFIA AVES

II

First Edition

Published by Little Quail Press

Cover Art by JS Designs

Editing Services provided by Heather Osborne

ISBN: 9781922448347